Picture
Perfect

Kelly McKain

USBORNE

My
totally secret
journal

by

Lucy Jessica Hartley

Saturday the 7th of May,
sitting on my bed
getting ready to do
some thinking.

Hi girls!

I'm starting this new journal 'cos I've got lots of thinking to do, and when lots of thoughts start buzzing round in my head I have to write them down so I can actually *see* what I'm thinking, if you get what I mean. And then I can think about it.

All my thinking is to do with Tilda, who is my fab **BFF** (**BFF** means Best Friend Forever, **BTW**). (**BTW** means By The Way, **BTW**.)

Firstly Tilda wants us three (that's me and her and my other **BFF** Julietta Garcia Perez Benedicionatorio, most usually known as Jules) to go to this meeting on Monday for the new school mag. We got handed these flyers about it in English last week.

5

Got something to say?

Come along to the English room at 12.30

on Monday 9th May to find out how

YOU can get involved in our

Wicked New School Mag!

WORD!

Oh dear, this is
Mr. Wright trying to be
down wid da kidz.
Cringe!

Eeeeeekkkkkk!!!! No one who
wears faded cords and a
jacket with leather patches
on the sleeves should be
allowed to say that!!!!!

Tilda is really brainy so she's into doing
lunchtime activities, like, for example, she already
has piano twice a week. For *my* lunchtime activity
I like to go in the loos and try out different make-

up and hairstyles with Jules. Mrs. Stepton our science teacher calls this *Vacuous Activity* and always shoos us outside for our *Fresh Air and Exercise*, and I have to explain to her that as my life's ambition is to be a *Real Actual Fashion Designer*, trying out hairstyles and make-up is way more important than hanging around in the playground trying not to get hit by tennis balls, which the boys use as footballs, 'cos they're not allowed actual footballs, 'cos they're dangerous, but in fact tennis balls are more dangerous due to being pingy and unpredictable when you kick them. Oh, dear, there were no full stops whatsoever in that whole bit. I hope you are reading this in your head, or you would have passed out from not breathing!

Anyway, we are all three going to the meeting because we are **BFF**, so we have to do important things together.

Tilda reckons we should spend the weekend thinking of what we could do on the mag using our *Unique Talents*. I want to do something about fashion, *of course*, but what? So I have got thinking to do for that, plus the thinking I have already got to do about Tilda's birthday, which is on the 14th of May, i.e. next Saturday, one week from now.

It is *soooooo* unfair that Tilda's going to be 13 when I'm not going to be it for 103 days, or that she has already got her Q when I'm still waiting for mine. (Q means period, **BTW**. We made up a secret code word so we can talk about it even when boys are there, and P sounded too obvious. Ingenious, huh?)

Jules has already been 13 for 93 days, but luckily she hasn't got her Q yet, so at least those two are not in a club of matureness without me. Oh, it would be *soooooo* amazing if my Q could just arrive right now, especially 'cos last week me and Jules were acting out telling our mums we'd got it, so now we're, like, *totally prepared*.

But to be honest it doesn't seem very likely to arrive soon because I am a *late developer* (as Mum and the assistants in Marks and Spencer's bra department call it – CRINGE!!!). That means I probably won't even get mine till I'm about 23 or something, and I'll be the oldest girl in the world who doesn't have it and my name will be in all the Record Breaker annuals that people get for Christmas and everyone will know I'm the latest starter ever, which will be just *soooooo* embarrassing!

Still, I suppose it isn't Tilda's fault she was born before me (and has started before me), so I am going to be very mature and forget being lime-green with envy and instead get on with planning a fab birthday happening for her.

Here are my ideas so far:

☆ What To Do For Tilda's Birthday ☆

1) Go shopping
2) Go out for pizza
3) See something at the cinema
4) Get loads of cool stuff from
   The Body Shop and then have a
   pampering sesh and makeovers
5) Have a sleepover

Hmmm, they all sound really fun, but I can't choose. The thing is that they don't seem **BIG** enough for something as important as your 13th birthday. After all, 13 is the magic doorway between being a *Very-Nearly-Teenager* and being an *Actual Teenager*. Teenager-ness is *the* most exciting time ever in your whole life, which is why adults keep wanting to be teenage *again*, which is why they say stuff like "wicked" and "word" and why my dad still wears leather trousers. I keep trying to tell him that they are in no way cool with the waistband of his ginormous pants sticking out the top, but he won't listen!

Oh, wow, I have just been struck with a

CREATIVE INSPIRATION

Flashes of inspiration!

I could throw Tilda a Surprise Birthday Party!

We can have cool drinks and food and music and games and dancing and everything! Maybe Mum'll even make Tilda a birthday cake if I ask really nicely and do flattery, like saying, "Wow, those trousers look great! You've really lost weight with all the stress of becoming a single parent!"

How totally fab will that be?!

Answer: Totally, totally fab!

I have also got some ideas of what present to get Tilda, which I wrote on a napkin in the Cool Cats café when I was waiting for Mum to come back from the ladies' loo, which is called *Dolls* in Cool Cats because it's all 50s style.

☆ **Ideas of What To Get Tilda** ☆

1. Juicy Jelly lipgloss (that'll stop her borrowing mine!)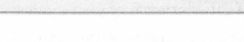
2. Purple glitter nail stars (then I can borrow hers!)
3. Pink jewelled mobile cover (she hasn't got a mobile, but she'll probably get one soon, because, like, everyone has.)
4. Bacon crisps ('cos her dad is very stricty and she's not allowed them at home.)
5. Pink bangles from New Look (just because!)

Oh, just a sec…

Sorry

for the interruptedness –
it is now 37 minutes later.

Someone was at the door, and Mum called out from the bathroom that she only had half her make-up on and could ⊥ go and I said, "I am in the middle of a very important thing," (i.e. writing in here!) and told Alex to get it (Alex is my little bro, BTW). But, of course, whenever he is playing Karate Kid on the Playstation in his room he becomes *Voluntarily Deaf*, so I had to go after all.

Sometimes when I'm galloping downstairs to answer the door I have secret imaginings about it being different cool people who have come to give me a *Life-Changing Experience*. Like, it could be someone who saw me modelling my Fantasy Fashion design on the catwalk, and they want to offer me a scholarship to fashion college in Paris and a dyed-pink poodle to take with me.

13

Or maybe Meg, this wardrobe mistress
I worked for on a Hollywood movie, would be
there saying, "Hey, Lucy, I've got a job to style a
pop video for Purple Seven in LA and there's no
way I can possibly do it without you," and I would
go, "Great, 'cos I have experience of styling a boy
band from when I did Blackstone for the school
rock concert in aid of charity."

In fact, I would even be happy if it was someone telling me I'd won a year's supply of fruit pastilles.

But it never *is* any of those cool happenings. Like, just now it was only Dad, coming round for "a chat" (which *actually* means helping himself to a sandwich, doing the crossword, and maybe asking to borrow the car).

I'm sure you know this by now, but just to quickly mention that Mum has become a Single Parent quite recently because Dad has decided to have this thing called a *Midlife Crisis*. I'm not sure what that is, but I asked Mum if it was a kind of illness and she went into tight-lippedness and said, "You could say that, yes."

Dad isn't covered in spots or anything, and he doesn't *look* sick. So I am thinking that the symptoms of a *Midlife Crisis* are less like measles and more like:

1) You leave your job as the manager of the local Sainsbury's because you want to become a rock and roll star.

2) You **CRUELLY ABANDON** your lovely family because you want to be 16 again.

3) You move to Uncle Ken's manky flat, which is up *4* flights of stairs with no lift, because you "need some space, man".

4) You stay indoors and strum your guitar all day while watching your *ginormous* pants drying on the radiator, because, erm, ???
⎯ *i.e. Who knows?*

Luckily Dad has recovered from symptom 4 now, 'cos he's got a job at our local radio station, which is called **WICKED FM**. At first he was just the running-around person, and his boss, Robert Hyde, wouldn't give him a chance of being a DJ, 'cos, well, he couldn't say so straight out, but basically 'cos he thought Dad was too old. Luckily I came up with this cool plan to prove to RH that Dad could do it, and it worked, and so he is about to start his new radio show.

So he should have been happy just now, but I knew something was wrong as soon as I *set eyes on him*.

He walked in and mumbled, "Hi, Lu, put the kettle on, will you?" Then he slumped down at the kitchen table and did a big dramatic sigh.

I was like, "What's up, Dad? You should be happy because your new radio show starts this week."

Dad groaned and went, "Yeah, but turns out that it sucks, man. I really thought I was getting the Drive-Time slot, from 5 to 7 p.m., because Robert kept talking about me entertaining people on their way home. But turns out he meant long-distance lorry drivers on their way home from delivering goods in Europe or something, because what I've actually got is not Drive Time but the Graveyard Shift."

I suddenly had this imagining of my dad doing his broadcast from an *actual* graveyard, and I totally did not get it, but then he explained that Graveyard Shift actually means the middle of the night, as in 10 p.m. to 2 a.m., when hardly anyone is listening.

Plus, Dad says the **L-DLD**s are mainly into country and western music so they won't like his show anyway, which is going to be rock, with a capital **R** (so, like, Rock).

This means Long-Distance Lorry Drivers, but I have shortened it to L-DLD 'cos writing it out is sooooooo yawn-making – but, oh no, I just wrote it out here by accident!

Mum had got all her make-up on by then, and she came downstairs. She frowned at me handing Dad a cup of coffee.

"Hi, Sue," he said, "any chance of a sandwich?"

Mum looked all harassed like she used to when he lived here and was constantly leaving the toilet seat up, but I quickly said, "Mum, I know you usually think that Dad should *Fend for Himself* 'cos when he's been here there's never anything left for our lunchboxes and also you're not *Made of Money*. But he is having another crisis like the midlife one so we should totally take pity on him, like the Good Samaritan."

Mum rolled her eyes and went, "Fine."

As I got the ham out, she said grumblingly to Dad, "Well, it'd better be a proper crisis, Brian. That's honey-roast from Marks's, you know."

So Dad explained about the Graveyard Shift and then Mum did think it was a bad enough crisis for him to eat our nice ham. "I don't even know *how* you're going to stay up that late," she told him, while buttering bread. "When we used to watch TV together you couldn't even make it beyond 10 o'clock without passing out on the sofa."

Dad got all huffity then and said, "That was passing out with *boredom*, not with *tiredness*, 'cos you always forced me to watch stuff like *Bridget Jones's Diary* or documentaries about women's problems."

Mum glared at him then. "When I think about the hours of football I sat through…" she began.

To stop them arguing, I sent Dad a secret look by darting my eyes rapidly between him and the ham sandwich Mum was making, meaning: *be nice or no more free food*. Luckily he got the hint and said soothingly to Mum, "Anyway, it's no hassle, the staying up. I'm a night owl, man. 10 o'clock's when I'm just warming up to hit the town and par-tay." Then he demonstrated by leaping up and doing some awful unfunky disco moves from ancient times (like, 1967 or something).

It is *soooooo* cringe-making that my dad thinks he's cool. Sometimes I wish I had a pipe-and-slippers-type dad like Tilda's, but then I wouldn't be allowed to have bacon crisps or a mobile, so maybe not.

After I had finished *dying* of embarrassment, and Dad had got his sarnie, I suddenly had a **REVELATION**. "You should make the most of the Graveyard Shift show because it might lead on to better things," I said. "After all, the running-around-man job led to you becoming a DJ, so if you do well at the Graveyard Shift, you might get given a better slot."

Dad thought about this (I could tell he was thinking because the ham sandwich paused in mid-air). "You're right, Lu. Positive thinking, that's what I need," he said eventually.

"Absolutely," added Mum. "You can't expect everything to land in your lap straight away, Brian. You have to work at things."

Dad pretended he didn't hear that, because it's what he calls being Nagged to Death, but he said thanks to me for the advice and helped himself to 2 Wagon Wheels for the walk home.

When I was waving Dad off, I was just thinking how cool it is that he stayed near us in Sherborne instead of going off around the world to be a roadie, and how he is actually quite okay for a dad. But then he spoiled it by doing his awful disco moves all the way down the street and actual people with eyesight were watching him.

Arrrrrrsssssshh!!!!!!!!!!!!!!

Monday after school

Sitting on my bed eating a banana, 'cos Dad polished off the last of the Wagon Wheels yesterday and now there is only fruit. Grrr!

I have had the most *fabulastic* day – the school magazine meeting turned out to be completely *fantablious*. I've got such a cool job to do on it – which I thought of in a *Creative Inspiration*, luckily.

What happened was, we were first to arrive at the English room (apart from Mr. Wright, of course), because Tilda made us stuff down our lunch so we wouldn't be late. She had this new spirally bound notebook and loads of really sharp pencils sticking out of her hair, which is apparently what journalists on real magazines have.

I went, "Don't get too excited, this will probably be as far away from a real magazine (i.e. my fab fave *Hey Girls!*) as it's possible to get. It will in fact most likely be full of *yawnoramic* stuff like reports of **PTA** meetings and inter-school football results and how much they raised in the tombola for the new IT centre. And Mr. Cain might even force us to write articles like, '*10 Top Tips for the Perfect Side-Parting*' and '*5 Ways to Shinier Shoes*' and maybe even some history like, '*The Life and Times of the Kipper Tie*'." (Mr. Cain is the *School Uniform Police* and my arch-enemy, **BTW**.)

Tilda threatened to poke me with one of her super-sharp pencils and said, "It'll be great, you'll see. I'm going to try for editor."

So anyway, some more people arrived, including Simon Driscott. Until recently I have been calling him the Prince of Pillockdom, but I don't any more since I found out that he is quite funny and okay, even with his strange lopsided haircut and weird hand signals from *Star Trek*. He only had one of his Geeky Minions with him for a change (usually there is this big group of clones trailing after him). Maybe they couldn't bear to leave the computer room (they hang round there every lunchtime even when it is not actual computer club, which is their *life's passion*).

If they could marry a computer they would!

The only time the **GM**s aren't in the computer room is when they're taking the mickey out of me for getting kissed by Simon Driscott in this film

I was recently in. They stupidly think it was because he has a crush on me, which is so silly when he only did it 'cos of having a *Creative Inspiration* that it would look good in the film. In real life we are just sort of friends with no fancying going on whatsoever.

After a few minutes of people arriving, Mr. Wright did that thing of hitching up his cords and sitting on the edge of his desk that English teachers think is cool. He explained that the mag was going to be "for the kids, by the kids", and he is just helping us with ideas and design, etc. So it *is* actually a real magazine and not just another way of Mr. Cain telling us what to do. It is also going to be called WORD!, which I didn't realize, but which is actually quite good considering it was made up by a teacher.

Tilda put her hand up and called out, "Can I be editor, please, Sir?" but Mr. Wright smiled and said, "Afraid not. I'm going to be that, so that I can monitor the content and style of the magazine, but I'm sure you'll come up with something excellent to contribute, Matilda-Jane." (The teachers still call

Tilda this, even though no one else does
since I gave her a fab makeover to turn her into a
super-cool babe!)

So Tilda really sadly took the super-sharp
pencils out of her hair then, 'cos she didn't know
what to be if she couldn't be the editor, and I had
to put my arm round her for a bit. Then we started
having a *Brainstorm*, which is not as painful as it
sounds, but more like thinking of ideas that could
go in the mag. Instead of putting our hands up like
normal we were allowed to shout our ideas out and
Mr. Wright wrote them all on the board.

Tilda cheered up when she had the idea of
doing an agony-aunt column called *Ask Tilda*.
Mr. Wright said it was good thinking because she
is so sensitive and mature *(v. v. true!)*. She made
a poster for it in the computer room at last break
(I did the pics!) and printed loads out, and then
me and Jules helped her stick them up round
the school. I printed a small size one to put in
here too.

Tilda Van der Zwan gives caring, practical advice
on all your problems, including friendships, boys,
schoolwork, bullying and family issues.
Just drop your letters into the "Ask Tilda" box outside
the secretaries' office and wait for your reply to
feature in the new school magazine!

Jules is doing a chat column called *Watch It!* about films she has most recently seen, because of her wanting to be an actress.

I had loads of fab fashion ideas, but none of them were *practical*, according to Mr. Wright. Like, he reckons the school can't afford to fly me to Italy for Milan Fashion Week (or even just Paris – the stingy-pants!). He also said no to me just simply interviewing Kate Moss in a posh hotel in London, or having a quiet dinner with Lily Cole. So when all my ideas had been horribly rejected I was just sitting there glumly wondering what fashion-y thing I could possibly do, when Simon Driscott said to me, "If you can't think of anything financially viable, Lucy, you can always help me out with my *Computer and Card-based Fantasy Game Review Column*."

I went, all sarkily, "Oooohhh, yes, please let me help you so I turn into a Geeky Minion and end up with a lopsided haircut, doing weird hand signals from *Star Trek*. That would be just great."

29

Simon shrugged and went, "Fine, whatever, only offering," totally normally, but with my *Female Intuition* I could tell I'd hurt his feelings – whoops! (I am following the instructions in my Teen Witch Kit to develop my *Female Intuition*. It mainly involves closing your two normal eyes and trying to look out of your *third* eye, which is somewhere in the middle, apparently, but actually invisible. I am practising most days, but my forehead keeps getting in the way at the moment.)

Plus, I thought about spending most lunchtimes on my own with no **BFF** while they worked on the mag, and Simon's offer didn't seem so bad after all. So I was about to say yes to doing the *Geeky Game column* thingie when I had the sudden *Creative Inspiration* I said about before. "I've got it!" I shouted out. "I could do my own fashion shoot right here in Sherborne! And instead of Kate Moss and Lily Cole and that, we can have models from this school, and instead of Stella Boyd designs we can get clothes from, erm, well I haven't decided that yet, but instead of Milan or Paris I can find a location in the town, and we'll get a photographer and everything, and we can lay it all out in the mag with writing that sets the scene and tells you about the style, and—"

"Lucy, breathe," said Mr. Wright, because I was going a tiny bit purple with the excitement.

"*Huuuuuurrrrrrrrrrrrr!*" I went, breathing.

"It's a great idea, but you'll need a partner," he said then, when I had returned to my usual colour.

"*I'll* do it," said Simon Driscott.

I whirled round and stared at him in GOBSMACKED FLABBERGASTATION. "But you don't care about fashion whatsoever," I stammered, feeling utterly confused.

"Maybe not," he said, in a James Bond kind of voice. "But I do have a brand-new top-of-the-range digital camera — and I know how to use it."

Everyone laughed at his joke and that sort of made me want to work with him after all. "Okay, then, you're hired," I said. "We'll have to get planning right away! I'll start scouting for locations and sorting out the clothes and—"

"Huh-hum," went Mr. Wright, doing that pretend-clearing-your-throat thing. "May I continue with the meeting, Lucy? I mean, if it's all right with you, of course!"

"Yes, Sir," I said, immediately getting the hint to stop talking. (See – it's not just Tilda who is sensitive and mature!) Still, I had to sit on my hands to stop myself making notes about the fashion shoot, 'cos ideas kept popping into my head.

So then Mr. Wright explained about how we could use the English room at lunchtimes to do our own bits of work on the mag and how we must all have everything ready by the deadline (which is Monday the 16th of May, 'cos the mag goes to press on the Tuesday morning). We are designing it on the Macs in the computer room, with help from Mr. Wright to lay things out and crop pictures and do scanning in and all that. Not that us two will need it, 'cos like I said, Simon Driscott's *life's passion* is computers.

And then that was IT, and the meeting was over, and I was packing up my stuff and slicking on some Strawberry Burst lipgloss and finding my long-lost Sparkle Babe nail polish down the lining of my bag, when Simon Driscott came up to me and boomed, "Captain Driscott at your service, Ma'am. Ready and waiting to receive instructions."

I said, "Right, well, I'll sort out some stuff for the shoot and get back to you with a schedule ASAP," (which is short for As Soon As Possible, BTW, and is cool 'cos it sounds business-y and professionalistic).

Simon clicked his heels together and said, "Yes, Ma'am," while doing a weird salute thing and then he did *Purposeful Striding* out of the room, like army men do on these old war films my dad likes.

So I have got gazillions to do, like having some

specified ideas for *Clothes* and *Locations*. Luckily
I have already had an idea for *Models*. You can
guess that I straight away asked Jules and Tilda to
be them. Jules wants to, but Tilda says she doesn't
think she's pretty enough (**NOT** true!!!) and also
that she would just feel awkward trying to act
grown-up in ultra-trendy clothes. So she
is going to be the dresser instead,
which means helping us do up
zips and running up with a
powder puff at the last minute
to retouch our make-up and that.

Oh, and great news about the Surprise
Birthday Party too! In computers I did secret
e-mailing with Jules and told her all about it, and
she thought it was a fab idea and so we are going
to start planning it straight away! *Yippeeeeee!!!!!!*

Of course, we were meant to be working on
our *Web-based cross-curricular personal
research projects*, but Mr. Webster the student
teacher usually reads *What Car?* mag at his desk

and never checks our screens as long as we are quiet. Tilda usually e-mails with us too, but of course we were talking about the Surprise Birthday Party, so we couldn't copy her in. So it was a bit scary after the lesson because Tilda just said straight out, "What were you two e-mailing about, and why didn't you include me?"

I was thinking Eeeeeekkkkkk!!!!!, but Jules quickly said, "We weren't e-mailing. We were doing our web-based cross-curricular personal research projects."

"That sounds highly unlikely," said Tilda sniffily.

"We *were*," I insisted. "We are totally into, er, you know, *learning stuff* now. *Information Technology* is a unique opportunity to explore the wonderful world of knowledge that can be brought to our fingertips simply by the double click of a mouse. OW!"

I shouted OW! because Jules had kicked my ankle, which I realized meant "Shut up!", so I just glared at her (it was a hard kick!) and zipped my lips.

"Oh, right," said Tilda sadly, and then she trailed off down the corridor without even waiting for us.

"Next time, Lu, leave the acting to me," hissed Jules.

It's awful making Tilda feel upset, but we just **CANNOT** let her find out about the Surprise Birthday Party. I can't wait to see her face when she walks in and sees all her friends and the fab food and balloons and everything. She will just be so totally over the moon!

Yikes, it's nearly half 5, which is when I have to go down and help make dinner, so I'd better stop writing in here. Hopefully while I'm chopping the carrots I'll have some fabby ideas to make a great fash splash in the mag!

Tuesday evening...
well, what's left of it!

I have just now finished a ginormous pile of homework (groan!). Don't the teachers know I've got more important things to do in the evenings? I mean, we already have school *all day*, taking up our time. At least I was able to sneakily make a list in maths of what I need to sort out for the photo shoot, so I managed to get *something* useful done.

Fashion shoot stuff

1) Great location
2) Great clothes
3) Great accessories
4) Great models (well, I've got one, I need one more)
5) Great hair and make-up design
6) Most of all - a great THEME

A theme is like, say, "Old-style New York" or "Picnic in the Woods" or "70s Disco" or whatever. I have been looking in my fash mags for inspiration. I've cut out these cool pics to show you some ideas, like:

You can do joy-of-livingness by running along a beach in white trousers

38

You can do cool summer
style by pouting in
sunglasses

When I was trying to get Mum to write me
an excuse note about my homework so I could
get on with my photo-shoot planning (she wouldn't
– *grrr!*), I told her about the clothes problem.
I mean, I have got a few nice things, but they
wouldn't fit Jules, and I am definitely not having
Goth Rock as the theme, so Jules's own clothes
are a no-no. Also, even if I could afford the material
(which I can't) there's no way I would have time

to make all the outfits, especially when the mag goes to press next Tuesday (i.e. in only one week's time!).

I was telling all this woe to Mum and she had the fab idea of us asking if we could borrow the clothes from this cool boutique in town called Girlsworld. So I've got the shop number out of the Yellow Pages and I'm going to ring up tomorrow at break and see what they say.

Fingers crossed for me!!!

Wednesday breaktime,
in the loos, touching up my
Luscious Lime lipgloss and
feeling very professionally efficient.

Great news – I just rang the Girlsworld shop from the secretaries' office and spoke to this lady called Cindy who runs it (Mr. Wright spoke to her too, for added officialness). She _loves_ the idea of the photo shoot and she's happy to lend us clothes for it as long as we are really, _really_ careful (and we mention the shop in the mag, of course!). Me, Jules and Tilda are going down there after school to check out her stock. How cool is that?!

Also, I was on the phone to Jules last night making plans for Tilda's Surprise Birthday Party, and we have decided we really want to have it round mine. So this morning I picked the best time to ask Mum about it, which was when she was most likely to say yes, which was when she was not really listening, which was when she was halfway round the big roundabout at the top of town with one of those weird blady tractors veering out in front of her.

I said there would only be about 10 people at the most and that we wanted to have it at mine because she (Mum) is so cool (TRUE!). Plus, she is the best person to supervise (no, I am not dense enough to think that my mum will go out and let us have a party all by ourselves!). Also, 'cos of reading *Raising Teenagers: The Most Rewarding Years* she knows not to make us do musical chairs or anything embarrassingly babyish like that.

And the amazing good news is that Mum said yes, okay, seeing as it's half term and Tilda's so nice, but not to ask her things while she's getting cut up by a combine harvester (so that's what it was!) or we most likely won't make it till Saturday alive.

So we are all systems go – *whoopee!!!!*

Me and Jules did have another *Eeeeeekkkkkk!!!!!!* moment with Tilda this morning, though. We had gone into the cloakrooms before school to do some Surprise Birthday Party planning. We were meant to only be whispering, but when I told Jules about Mum saying yes she got all excited and yelled out, "Wicked!" really loud, and that made me get excited too so that we were both jumping up and down squealing when Tilda came in.

"Who's that?" she called.

I thought *GULP!* and we quickly hid under the *ginormous* duffel coats of Simon Driscott and the Geeky Minions and tried to stand very still, but Tilda rummaged around until we were revealed. "Oh, it's you two," she said surprisedly. "Erm, why aren't you in the loos like usual?"

"We were hiding from you!" I blurted out, because it was the honest truth, but then Jules kicked me hard (again!) and I realized it sounded not very nice.

"We, er, I, er, it's a new game..." Jules said actingly. "I thought Lucy told you."

"Oh, yeah, and I thought *Jules* told you," I went, catching on to the clever fib.

43

Tilda didn't say anything else, so I think we got away with it.

"Anyway, it's nearly the bell, we'd better go in," said Jules quickly. So we detangled ourselves from the duffel coats and each grabbed one of Tilda's arms and steered her down the corridor. As we were going along, Tilda said, "I was thinking, maybe, for my birthday…"

So that was another *Eeeeeekkkkkk!!!!!!* moment, with added *Yikes!* Of course, we can't talk about Tilda's birthday in case the top secret party info slips out by accident. I managed to change the subject on to what happened in *Neighbours* last night, and she forgot all about it – **phew!** I suppose we should have made up a pretend birthday plan, like, say, one of the things off my list, but we didn't think of it.

Oh, that's the bell, better get going I suppose. It would be a waste of me bothering to copy Jules's maths homework if I'm going to be in trouble with Mr. Bridges anyway for being late.

At home

on Wednesday night. Lots of interesting things have happened since I wrote in here this morning!

The first interesting thing was that me and Jules and Tilda went to Girlsworld. I sometimes go in there to look on a Saturday, so I'd seen some of the stuff before, but Cindy had some great new lines, too, like these fab Capri pants which are halfway between normal trousers and shorts, and are quite skinny round your legs, like

And she also had these cool dresses that go in at the waist with a belt so that even people like me with hardly any hips or you-know-whats look grown-up-ly womanly.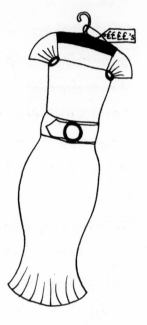

It's quite expensive, as in more like asking-for-your-birthday than paying-with-your-pocket-money type thing, so I could see why we had to be really, *really* careful with the clothes.

Cindy was *soooooo* nice – she's offered to lend us 3 different outfits for each model – how cool is that?! It was tricky to know what we'd actually use until we got a location and theme. I was hoping seeing the clothes would give me some ideas, but I didn't have any *Creative Inspirations*. Cindy says I can pop back and decide what I need later in the week, though, so that was okay.

Then we went to have a look at locations, and I was hoping to get inspired by a theme then too. We trailed round town and looked at the abbey and the market cross, but nothing was exactly fashion-shoot-ish and it was all more like old-ladies-having-afternoon-tea-ish. I wish we lived in London where it is all vintage clothes markets and giant billboards and people going "*Gor blimey, guv'nor*" while riding their scooters around Big Ben. That would be way more fashion-inspiring!

Then it started raining really hard and we had to run for shelter into the Cool Cats café, which is my fave place since I decided to start hanging out in coffee shops like they are always doing on TV. So we ended up wet and cold and location-less, huddled into a booth with these cool red leather bench things, sharing a small hot chocolate because our money all put together was only £1.28p. Tilda called her dad on Jules's mobile and asked him to come and get us and he said okay. When she rang off, she held onto the mobile for a

47

long time, obviously wishing she had one herself, until Jules asked for it back.

While we were waiting to get picked up, Tilda pulled out a wodge of *Ask Tilda* letters from her bag. "Wow, that's a lot!" I went. "And it's only been 2 days! How cool that so many people wrote in! You must be totally *skipping through the tulips!*"

I am using this to mean "over the moon" instead of actually saying "over the moon". I like making up new phrases, so I don't have to keep using the same old boring ones all the time!

"Erm, I suppose so," she sighed, not sounding very tulip-skippy at all. "It's, just, people have more problems than I thought. There's no way all these will fit in the school magazine, but I can't bear to leave anyone without advice, so I'm writing back to everyone and pinning my replies up on the noticeboard outside the dining hall."

I stared at the pile of letters. "You're replying to *all* these?" I said, gasping in amazement.

"It looks like hard work," said Jules, slurping more than her share of the hot chocolate until I gave her a hard nudge.

"It is, but as long as it helps people, I don't mind," said Tilda. She is really sweet and kind like that. Maybe it's 'cos her mum died when she was only little, so she feels even more sorry than normal for upset people, if you get what I mean. Or maybe she's just always been a really, really extra-nice person.

"Look, we've still got to find a location for the fashion shoot that is cool and trendy, yet quirky and individual," I said, suddenly panicking. "Think, girls, think!"

So we all had a hard think but no ideas came. We must have used them all up in the Brainstorming thing on Monday.

I went, "I can't help feeling like the answer is staring me right in the face, if only I could see it." And then I realized I was gazing at the marble counter and the chrome soda fountain, which is

49

only for decoration now, but still, and I had the
REVELATION that the answer was ACTUALLY
staring right into my face – or I was staring right
at *it*, more like!

"We can use the café!" I blurted out. "We can
do a cool 1950s theme but adapted to modern
girls! We can use those Capri pants (remember the
three-quarter-length trousers I said about?) and
gorgeous shirts… Oh, I know, we can tie them up
at the front, like they do on *Grease*, in fact the
theme can BE *Grease*, as in the film, not as in
what Dad got covered in when he recently tried
to fix Mum's car, and we can find some cool
platforms and maybe Cindy will lend us that lovely
cinched-waist dress if we promise to be absolutely
completely careful!! We can do shots up at the
counter and in one of these red leather booths and
by the bubblegum machine, and I'll get Mum to
show me how to do that sweepy-eyeliner thing
they all used to have, *etc., etc., etc.*"

↑
This is me going on so much
I can't even write it all out!

50

At first Jules and Tilda were just staring at me, probably trying to get my babblingness to sink into their brains, and then they started getting enthusiastic.

Jules went, "And the models can be sipping huge ice-cream sodas and maybe even eating cheese sandwiches."

"How are cheese sandwiches 1950s?" asked Tilda.

"They're not, I just like them," said Jules. It's true — almost every time she's round mine she quickly has a cheese sandwich before we do *anything*.

I didn't even hear them saying suggestions after that because I was up at the counter like a bullet asking the owner (who apparently is called Reggie) if we could use the café for our fashion shoot. I first of all asked for Saturday, but he said no, 'cos it's too busy then, and no to Friday too, but he did offer for us to come tomorrow after school.

"Yikes!" I cried. "That's hardly any time to organize it at all!"

He shrugged, going, "That's all I can do, and it's on condition that you don't disturb any of the other customers and that the café gets a credit in the mag."

So I agreed and that was cool and all sorted!

When I told the girls, Tilda was really disappointed 'cos she has piano tomorrow after school and she absolutely has to go because she's being put in for her Grade 6 or whatever (she is *really* good) so she won't be able to be the dresser after all.

"Don't worry," I said helpfully, not wanting her to feel bad, "we can manage without you."

"Oh, erm, great," mumbled Tilda.

Then I was struck by a sudden horror. "Oh, no, model crisis!" I cried. "There isn't time to find anyone!"

"Why don't *you* do it?" Tilda suggested. "Then it can be just you and Jules, all cosy together

52

as a two." She seemed a bit grumpy – it must have been the stress of all the *Ask Tilda* letters.

"Brilliant! Fab idea!" I cried, wondering why I hadn't thought of it before. I suppose I was concentrating on being the stylist and director, but of course I can be the model as well. "Thanks, Tilda! You're such a great **BFF**!" I cried.

"You're welcome," she said and carried on with her letters, not looking at me.

When Tilda's dad came, he bought us a proper size hot chocolate each – he is very nice although very old-fashionedly stricty, and strangely I find my voice going posher whenever I talk to him.

When I got home I looked up Simon's number and rang him about doing the shoot tomorrow. He said he can, even though he will have to miss *Fantasy Role-playing Club* – the Geeky Minions will just have to cope without their leader for once – hee hee! Mum even said she will lend us her **MAC** make-up, as long as we are very, very, very careful

Why does everyone keep saying that? Of course we will be!

and only use a little bit and don't mix up the brushes and do give it to the secretary to look after till home time… (There was like a 20-minute lecture about this, which I had to listen to and just go, *Yeah, yeah, yeah,* but lucky for you I am not writing it all down!)

So it is all sorted – *yippeeeeee!!!!!!*

Right, I absolutely must go now and think about poses and make-up and outfits.

Byeeeeee!!!

Thursday
after having a pre-production
meeting with Simon Driscott.

*Meaning before we
do the fashion shoot*

I just have to tell you that the meeting was
soooooo great! Mr. Wright loved the idea for the
shoot and said I really had "*my finger on the
fashion pulse*" and that I was also "*very
talented*"! I would never write that about myself
normally, 'cos of sounding like a big-head, but that
is what he honestly said.

Simon Driscott loved the theme too, but when
I was showing him my detailed plans for the poses
and costumes and make-up and accessories and
that, he went a bit spacey, like he was not in fact
listening. I nudged him hard and said, "You're
supposed to be concentrating. This is vitally
important information!"

"Oh, but I thought I just had to point and
shoot," he went. "As you said, I have no interest

in fashion whatsoever, so why would you want my opinion?"

"Well, because we're doing it together, aren't we?" I said annoyedly. "We're a team so we should be consulting each other about stuff – that's how fashion professionalists work."

"You mean professionals," said Simon Driscott, doing that thing of correcting me he always does that drives me absolutely round the bend. "And yes, you're right, we're a team. Okay, then, explain it to me again." He pointed to the Capri pants on one of my drawings. "Are those bizarre items trousers or shorts?"

I rolled my eyes that someone could know almost the entire dictionary and yet be so completely uneducated about such **VITAL** issues of life as trouser lengths, but I am letting SD off because at least he is trying to learn.

And after that we were basking in our glow of teaminess so much that I persuaded Simon to design Tilda's Surprise Birthday Party invitations on one of the computers (I myself am rubbish at computer designing, so I just directed what he was doing).

I was worried she might walk over and spot what we were up to, but she was so buried in a big pile of *Ask Tilda* letters she hardly looked up all lunchtime.

The invites are so cool, like this:

Surprise Birthday Party (ssshhhh)!!!

Dear _____

Please come and celebrate Tilda's birthday

On: Saturday 14th May
From: 7 p.m. — 9.30 p.m.
At: 4 The Meadows, Barnaby Road,
    Sherborne (which is Lucy Jessica
    Hartley's house)
    RSVP to Lucy or Jules, Form 8P
    PS Don't let the secret slip to Tilda!

After school Tilda is at her piano lesson, so me and Jules are quickly giving the invites out before we head down to Girlsworld to collect the clothes for our shoot. We're inviting all Tilda's friends from Extended Maths and the other lunchtime piano players and Augusta Rinaldi's lot (but definitely not Gina Fulcher, who was a massive bully to Tilda when she first started at our school, so she's not coming, so there!) and all the okay boys from our class, like Ben Jones and Bill Cripps and Jamie Cousins.

I'm also inviting Simon Driscott for being such a fab team with me on the fashion pages (and also because he has a mobile disco and has offered to be in charge of music) and I suppose the Geeky Minions will have to come as well as they are virtually unseparate-able from him.

So, hmm, that is more than the 10 I told Mum, but then I did just say "about 10" and not give an actual exact number, so it should be okay. If you think about it 27 people is definitely way closer to 10 people than say 2,094 people, so she shouldn't really mind.

Oh, the bell just went for end of break. Only one more double lesson before the fashion shoot. *Yessity-yes-yes!!!!!!*

Thursday night,
after the fab fashion shoot!!!

Wow, what a totally amazing experience!

Everything was cool beans at the shoot, and fingers crossed the pix will be really good. After giving out Tilda's party invitations, me and Jules went and picked out the clothes at Girlsworld (Cindy is just *soooooo* nice! I wish she could be my aunt and take me shopping and do my make-up and that!), and then we walked down to the Cool Cats café.

Simon was already there, setting up. Me and Jules had massive fun getting into the outfits in the ladies' loos and doing the 50s make-up and hair and everything. The only sad thing was that Tilda couldn't be there too, but we do understand about her piano.

For our first shot, we did "Casual", like this

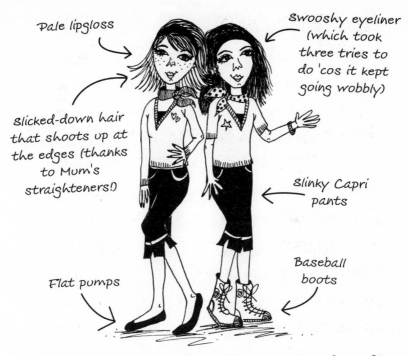

Pale lipgloss

Swooshy eyeliner (which took three tries to do 'cos it kept going wobbly)

Slicked-down hair that shoots up at the edges (thanks to Mum's straighteners!)

Slinky Capri pants

Flat pumps

Baseball boots

When we were ready we went out into the café and I asked Reggie for some Coke floats, which are the closest you can get to proper ice-cream sodas nowadays. Me and Jules planned to sit at the counter on stools, giggling like we were telling each other secrets (no problem with that, 'cos we've practised it loads over the last few years!). So we started styling the background, i.e. taking down the rack of Cheese Moments, which did not

look very 50s. It was all going really well until
I asked two tables of people to swap so we could
have the ones without hoodie tops on in the shot.
(Okay, well, less *asked* and more *swapped their
food round and dragged them across the café*
– but it's not my fault I'm perfectionistic, is it?!)

Anyway, Reggie got *soooooo* cross he started
looking like Mr. Cain does when he catches me
accidentally wearing my studded belt over my
uniform (i.e. like his feet were going to boil in his
shoes!). "I only said you could shoot in here if there
was no disturbance," he growled scarily. "One more
foot out of line and you're banned!"

That was unfortunate, because just then one more
foot did go out of line (Simon's) as he tripped up the
waiter and orange juice flew through the air and the
tray went clanging down. I said, "Sorry, sorry, sorry,"
to Reggie loads of times, and he grumbled, "One
more chance, but stay out of my way!"

Phew! So I grabbed the Coke floats and
steered Simon and Jules into a red booth right at the

back of the café. And that's where we ended up doing the shots. It was really good in the end and made me think how sometimes as a stylist and director you have to do quick thinking and decide things *as the action unfolds* (so it was all great training for my future career as a fashion designer!).

Simon took loads of pictures, going snap-snap-snap like a real professional photographer, and he had this great idea of making us look away and then only up at the camera at the last minute, so we didn't have those scary fixed grins on our faces you always get in school photos. Me and Simon made a good team, mainly 'cos of me deciding what we should do and him simply doing it without arguing. Jules was fab too, because even though she is very argue-y in real life, when she is in front of a camera she acts totally *professionalistic* and does exactly what you say, 'cos she sees it as training for her life-long ambition of being an actress. I wish people just did what I wanted all the time in real life without arguing – *how totally cool would that be?!*

For the second look, we had decided to be dressed as sort of cheerleaders, 'cos we borrowed these cool red miniskirts from Girlsworld and we already had some silver pompoms made out of glitter wigs from Mum's work's Christmas party. I styled us like this:

High ponytail with backcombing and lots of hairspray to give it height

"Barely there" make-up

Glitter wig pompoms

50s sports jacket

Cute white vest top

Red pleated miniskirt

Little white socks and white trainers (mine are a bit big 'cos I borrowed them off Mum, who bought them for tennis and only played once!)

When I came out in my cheerleader outfit, Simon Driscott took one look at me and dropped his tripod, so I knew I must look *stunningly groovy* 'cos usually he is *Immune to style*. Then Jules came out and we were ready to shoot.

I tried to think of how to get action in the shots to make it more exciting but without hardly moving at all in case we annoyed Reggie and blew our last chance. So I had the idea to take the pictures next to the cool bubble gum machine.

Jules had a great idea, which was to get some bubblegum out of the machine and blow bubbles as big as possible for Simon Driscott to catch on camera. We got all set up and each blew a massive bubble, but for some weird reason Simon Driscott didn't take the shot, and was instead fiddling with something on his camera.

65

Me and Jules kept blowing the bubbles and Simon
Driscott kept **NOT** taking the pictures until –

Yurgh! The bubbles burst all over our faces
and all the customers laughed and clapped and
that made Simon finally concentrate and that's
when he took a picture, like this:

Me and Jules were totally embarrassed, but
Reggie was happy at least, because we were
entertaining his customers instead of annoying
them! So we had to peel all the pink gum off our
faces in the loos and then redo our make-up, 'cos
even though it was the "barely there" style it takes
loads of products to get such a natural look. And
there's no way that shot going in the mag!

The final outfit was the most fun and also the
most amazing transformation of us into looking
about 18. I *soooooo* wish I could afford to buy
the dress I wore and then every time I put it on
I would remember the shoot and feel utterly
amazing, but no way will that ever happen 'cos
it's far too expensive.

We put the black liquid eyeliner on again, but
much thicker this time, and we did more of a
swoop out to the side of our eyes, like this

We also had this foundation Mum lent me that she said Nan left behind after staying over, which is called panstick, and this loose powder you put on with a big poofy thing and this bright red lipstick of Mum's that I would never normally be allowed to borrow because she says it's unsuitable for girls my age.

In the end we looked like this:

Lovely glammy make-up →

Pouty red lips →

Roland-Mouret-style hourglass dress (wow – I have some actual curves in this!)

Extra special high heels borrowed from Mum ↘

Cool hairdos called chignons, which Mum told me are totally 50s and showed me how to do

Cool vintage-style cinched-waist dress

Heels borrowed from Jules's mum (Jules doesn't own any as she is normally in DMs)

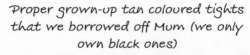
Proper grown-up tan coloured tights that we borrowed off Mum (we only own black ones)

When we'd got everything on, we felt totally glammy, like film stars, and we couldn't stop staring at ourselves in the mirror. We were taking so long that Simon Driscott had to knock on the door of the loos and tell us to hurry up 'cos he'd had a fab idea. When we came out he said, "Why don't we ask Reggie to draw the blinds and light the candles? They'll be really twinkly on camera. And perhaps we could even persuade him to put on the glitter ball for some evening glamour."

We all looked up at the big silver ball hanging from the ceiling, which is normally just for decoration, but you can switch it on so it turns. It was a fab idea, but I couldn't see Reggie doing us any favours! Then, to my amazement, as the café hadn't started filling up for the evening yet and the afternoon rush was over, he started being nicer to us. He said *Okay* about the blinds and candles and glitter ball and also that we could now do some shots sitting up on the stools at the counter if we were quite quick.

I said, "That's great, thanks, Reggie, but we have the small problem that sipping Coke floats will not look sophisticated and glammy enough to go with these outfits and plus we have already got them in the other shot."

Reggie had a think, and then he made us these cool cocktail-type drinks out of all different fruit juices and put them in triangle-shape glasses.

And, even better, they were free! Reggie turned the glitter ball on, and it was fab with all the little bits of light moving around the room. We sat at the counter with our legs crossed politely, acting like glam black-and-white-movie stars, sipping our

cocktails. Simon Driscott was click-click-clicking away and for a moment I let myself pretend that we were celebs having a posh night out and being caught on camera by ~~paparazzi~~ ~~parparzari~~ ~~paparazzi~~ photo-journalists. *Must learn how to spell that word!*

Then Simon was finished, and we pulled the blinds up and I came back to reality. Me and Jules finished our fake cocktails, which were completely delish, and I am definitely doing them for Tilda's Surprise Birthday Party!

Then that was **IT** and the fashion shoot was over and it was very nearly 6.30 p.m., which is when Mum was picking us up. It has honestly been one of the most fun days of my life! When I think about doing this *all* day *all* the time for my whole actual *career* it makes my stomach go *swoozy* and my head go *whoosh* with total excitement!!!

Jules went straight to the loos to get her make-up off, but I hung round while Simon Driscott was packing up his stuff and said well done and how I thought we were a great team. Also, because he didn't get a fake cocktail, I added, "Let me buy you a hot chocolate to say thank you."

But Simon said he had to go home straight away because three Geeky Minions were arriving very soon for a *Star Trek* DVDathon. (Well, he didn't *say* Geeky Minions, of course, he said their actual names, which I can't remember now, but anyway...)

"Well, maybe I can buy you a drink when we're at Tilda's party," I said. "Oh, except they'll be free, of course, but I could, erm, hand you one or something, and maybe stand there while you drink it."

Simon gave me a strange look that I didn't

entirely get. "When *we're* at Tilda's party?" he repeated. "You mean, *together*?"

He was obviously confused from the swirling of the glitter ball. "Of course we'll be together," I repeated slowly and clearly, like I have to when Mum's tired after work and she asks me the same question about 7 times. I mean, obviously the party is at my house, so it would be a bit strange if I wasn't actually *there*, wouldn't it?

Simon was beaming like, erm, the sun and a lighthouse put together, and going, "Great, well, pick you up at 8! And don't be late!"

I was going, "Huh?" so he said, "Well, not 8 but 7, and clearly I won't be picking you up to escort you to your own house because that would be absurd – I was in fact making reference to the Big Bopper's 1958 hit "Chantilly Lace" for the purpose of, you know, 50s-themed comedy."

"Oh, right," I said. I *soooooo* did not get that, but anyway.

Jules was calling me into the loos to help her

73

with a stuck zip and when we came out again, Simon had already dashed off to his Geekathon, or whatever it was. Mum came and we dropped the Girlsworld clothes back to Cindy's actual flat above the shop, 'cos she'd closed up for the night. We kept gabbling on about how fab the shoot was and saying zillions of thank yous till Mum had to almost drag us back to the car.

So now I'm back here and it's after tea, and even though it was my fave, lasagne, I still took ages eating it 'cos I was busy telling Mum and Alex about the fashion shoot. Oh, I can't believe it is over! Still, I hope it is only the first one I do in my life and there'll be many more to come. And anyway, no time to be sad about that, because there is loads to do for Tilda's Surprise Birthday Party. So I'm off to start planning right now!

Friday the 13th

Unlucky for some, but not for me 'cos I'm having loads of cool ideas for how to lay out the fashion pages — hee hee!!!

NOT SO UNLUCKY 13TH!

My ideas are:

<u>Main title:</u> Cool Cats!

<u>Intro copy:</u> Grab your blue suede shoes and have fun with our 50s-style fashion feature!

This is what you call the words, BTW

<u>Subtitle:</u> Diner Babes!

<u>Copy:</u> Hang out in cool casuals with a 50s twist! Pair snug slim-fit sweaters in lemon, baby blue or soda pink with slinky black Capri pants — perfect with pumps for daytime or smarten up the look with your Special Occasion high heels for instant glamour!

Then we'll have "Get the Look" boxes after each pic that say, like, trousers and top at whatever price they are from Girlsworld and *shoes, model's own,* that sort of thing. Also:

Huh! I was so busy sitting in bed writing my *copy* that Alex got downstairs first and nabbed the last of the Coco Pops, so I have been left with Shredded Bran, which tastes like hamster bedding and each mouthful takes about 5 minutes and 42 seconds to chew. But I don't care, 'cos I'd rather have cool ideas than Coco Pops, which shows my total journalistical dedication to the mag.

Urgh!

Back at home,
back at the kitchen table, but after school!

Well, I can now tell you that the pictures came out absolutely fab-ly and there are plenty of great shots to choose from. Simon brought them in on a CD and got them up on a Mac to show me – how techno-tastic is that?!

Jules had a quick look and said how cool she thought they were, but then she was busy with her *Watch It!* column so it was just me and Simon on our own. Between *some* girls and *some* boys that might be a bit awkward-feeling, but luckily we are just sort of friends, so it was fine and more like just hanging round normally with girls.

Tilda was there answering a giant pile of *Ask Tilda* letters, and trying to choose which ones to put in the actual mag, and when I offered to show her the photos she said she didn't have time. She sounded a bit huffity, but I didn't get annoyed 'cos I understand that she is very stressed out with having so much *Ask Tilda* stuff to do.

Simon loved my *copy* too and showed me how to type it into a file on the Mac. We even drew a rough layout on paper, to show where everything is going, and have half decided which pix we are using.

He thinks he can even cut out and enlarge the glitter ball and use it as our background so the whole two pages will look all sparkly and twinkly! We're going to put it all together on Monday (well, *he* is, of course, being the computer geek – whoops, I mean, the computer *genius*).

Mr. Wright came over to see what we were doing and he said the pix were really good and that it was "all shaping up nicely". But just at that second Mr. Cain came striding in to tell Mr. Wright about how he thought the Year 10 production of *Macbeth* should be performed in full school uniform, so we got interrupted.

I could tell Mr. Wright was trying not to laugh,

but he said seriously, "That's an interesting postmodern concept, Mr. Cain, and I'll certainly consider it."

But then – YEEK! – Mr. Cain glanced at our roughs and layouts and the minute he spotted our cheerleader pix with the miniskirt outfits he went completely *apoplectic* with rage, which means so angry your eyes are almost actually *popping out.* "Mr. Wright, surely you cannot be allowing that sort of frivolity into the school magazine?" he stammered.

"This magazine is 'for the kids, by the kids'," said Mr. Wright, "and as I don't consider this content to be offensive of course I'm allowing it."

Mr. Cain did a *snort of derision.* "But there are standards, Mr. Wright!" he snapped. "And by kids, I assume you mean *children*, rather than baby goats?"

Me and SD had to really clamp our lips together to keep from laughing then.

Mr. Wright just smiled at him. "Yes, isn't it wonderful how language changes and evolves all the time?" he said.

Mr. Cain just snorted again and marched out.

Mr. Wright turned to us, "Don't worry about him, *kids*," he said pointedly. "Your pages are great. Just keep going the way you are – and you'll have it all ready for the end of Monday, won't you?"

"Yes, Sir," we both said at once. It's true, I had been wondering a bit what Mr. Cain would say about the miniskirts, seeing as how he's so stricty about our school skirts being down by our knees. But with Mr. Wright sticking up for us, no way can Mr. Cain ruin our fashion pages!

When the bell went, we arranged to meet up at Monday morning break and lunch to work on our layout (how cool!).

Simon said, "But I'll see you before that too, won't I?" and did a wink at me.

I knew he was winking because Tilda was in the room and we couldn't say even one word about her Surprise Birthday Party, so I said, "Yep," and did a big wink back.

Me and Jules are doing well with the party

planning and I have even thought of a fab way to get Tilda round my house (tell you later). We have already arranged for Simon to bring his mobile disco, with flashing lights and everything – although *we* are choosing the music and not him in case it ends up as sci-fi-type theme tunes all night or something *(groan!)*. And Mum is taking us shopping on Saturday for the food and party decorations and things, so it is all mainly done, well sort of.

Tonight me and Mum are having a girly night in and we are staying up specially to listen to Dad's show too, which is mega-exciting – I can't wait to see what fab things he comes up with – I'm sure that by now he's totally popular with the listeners and that his boss will be giving him a better slot v. v. soon! I am in charge of making the Rice Krispie marshmallow cakes and setting up my foot spa and nail bar in the living room for later, so I'd better go and sort it out!

Saturday morning

No, wait, tick-tick-tick, Saturday afternoon!

We are all having a lazy ~~morning~~ afternoon after staying up so late, and we had a silly morning too 'cos we just had a competition to make the tallest bagel and mine was like this:

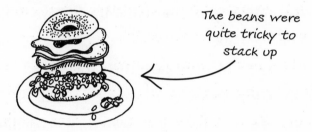

The beans were quite tricky to stack up

Alex actually won 'cos he put fried tomatoes in his (which I honestly can't stand). I'm writing this while I recover from my huge bagel, but I have to hurry 'cos Jules is coming round soon to go shopping with me and Mum and Alex for the party balloons and food and those popping things you can get where streamers shoot out.

We had lots of fun last night too, having foot spas and painting each other's toenails – Alex begged to have his done (just to get out of going to bed, I bet!) so we did them, and now he is going round with toes the colour of Magenta Magic! We scoffed a massive bowl of popcorn and loads of my Rice Krispie cakes, which came out all oozy, but Mum said, "Never mind," and also, "Anyway, it's more fun if you have to lick them off the paper!"

Plus, she said about how she's sorry she's always tired from work and stressed out all the time and that we should do more things together like this on the weekends to make up for it. I said maybe she should get a different job that she actually *likes*, and then she wouldn't be so stressed (my idea was retraining as a make-up artist, because right then she was doing my eyes in Mystical Allure plum shadow) and how it's not fair that Dad gets to be *fulfilled* and she doesn't. She

really laughed, not in a happy way, but more in a
Ha ha, very funny sarky way and said that with
Dad not earning much it was even more important
for her to have a secure job. It's so lucky I'm going
to be an *Actual Real Fashion Designer* when I
grow up, so I will be doing my favourite thing
from the second I leave college.

Also we had a *Friends* DVD on in the
background, and I even persuaded Mum to have a
go on my dance mat, which really made both of us
laugh. I am definitely putting it out at Tilda's party!
When it was 10 p.m. we put on Dad's show and
settled down on the sofa.

After a few minutes of listening Mum groaned
and said, "Oh no, I'd really been pinning my
hopes on your father becoming a famous DJ and
making some proper money, but clearly that is not
to be."

I didn't like hearing her say something not nice
about Dad, but I have to admit she was right that
the show was not very good. In fact, so many

things went wrong in it I have made a flowchart thingie to show you, like we do in science. (Mrs. Stepton would be pleased that I'm doing her subject in my spare time!)

Dad forgetting his cue

Dad eating something (a Twix, maybe?) loudly over the music, not realizing his mike was still on

Dad pacing about to keep awake

↓

Dad slurping some coffee (still not
realizing his mike is on!)

↓

Dad all jangly from the coffee, talking really
fast so you can't understand _what_ he's saying

So, even though I tried to look interested in the radio show out of loyalness to Dad, I fell asleep just after eleven and Mum had to wake me up and help me stumble up the stairs to bed.

To be honest (and I will only say this inside the pages of my totally secret journal) it was **REALLY** terrible. And I only heard one hour! Mum told me this morning that Dad also actually *fell asleep*, and after this one song ended all you could hear was snoring for about five minutes until Robert Hyde went crashing into the studio and slammed on some heavy metal really loud to wake him up!

Obviously my advice about positive thinking was not enough and I will have to help Dad make his show better, or he'll never get a prime-time slot and he'll be stuck on the Graveyard Shift forever and ever!

I know – I'll have a look in my Teen Witch Kit and see if it says anything about making awful DJs

into good ones! Oh, no time now, that'll be Jules
ringing the bell, but I'll do it after the party,
for sure!

Byeeeeee!!!!!!

<u>Only 1 hour and</u>
<u>22 minutes</u>

before people arrive for the party!

Jules has just now gone home again to change and I have just finished making Tilda a cool birthday card. I have drawn her in her fave hippy chick outfit and I've put actual fabric on it from my offcuts box. I am right now working on the message to put inside it. I am trying to do a rhyming one, but it is turning out to be quite tricky. Like, I have thought of:

To Tilda,
Wishing you the best birthday ever,
It's soooooo cool we're going to
celebrate it together,
I just know we will be
Best Friends Forever,
Even when we're like, 24 or something

massively old and I am living in New York and my designs are featuring in American Vogue and you are doing something vital like saving the endangered orang-utans of Borneo that we did about in citizenship. ←

You can see that the last line is not exactly rhyming, but at least it's what I want to say and not just something like "And you will stop eating bacon crisps never" that I could have put in just because it rhymes

The living room looks *soooooo* party-ish now. We moved the furniture to the edges and made a space for Simon Driscott to put his mobile disco. Mum took out her vase of flowers in case there are any accidents and I took out her selection of school photos of me in case anyone with actual eyes sees them (CRINGE!).

We got some cool balloons saying "Happy Birthday" and me and Jules kept blowing them up till our cheeks went really painful and then luckily Jules had the clever idea of paying Alex one Starburst sweet per balloon to do them for us. We have also put silver and purple streamer thingies all round the room and hanging down from the bunches of balloons. When Tilda walks in, she'll be *soooooo* happy!

When we were in town getting the party stuff, I also got my present for Tilda. I know how much she wants a mobile phone so I decided on the pink sparkly mobile case in the end. Then she can show it to her dad as a massivo hint and maybe he will buy her a phone to go in it. *Genius, huh?*

We have done a table of food in the kitchen (and Mum says it has to be eaten there and not taken into the living room, **OR ELSE!**) Honestly, parents! It's not like we're going to spill anything – after all, we're very-nearly-13 and very-actually-13, not 5.

For food we have got:

1. Tilda's fave bacon crisps, of course.

2. Pizza slices. (Mum says we can't just have crisps and cakes and that or people will be pinging off the ceiling, but I didn't want to do sandwiches or it will feel like being at school on packed lunches – i.e. **NOT** very party-ish!)

3. Sausages on sticks.

4. Cheese and pineappley things, also on sticks, that are **VITAL** at a party, even though it is two things that don't normally go together.

5. I have also been inspired to invent some canapés like the ones at the wrap party of this movie I was recently in. I am doing:

Dairylea avec cucumber à la Ritz cracker

Frazzle et Wotsit skewers (v. tricky to make!)

Surprise parcels (i.e. half a Babybel wrapped in wafer-thin ham)

6. Cool birthday cake that we made and decorated (well, okay, that Mum made and we decorated).

For drinks we have recreated the fruit cocktails that Reggie made us at the fashion shoot but I couldn't persuade Mum to buy the little umbrellas and swizzle sticks and glacé cherries to go in them, 'cos she said they were *an astronomical rip-off*. There is also Coke and Lemon Fanta for the *desperately unadventurous*, i.e. the boys.

MY WORST NIGHTMARE

is that if we only have music the boys won't dance and then we'll all be standing there at the sides of the room not talking to each other. So, I have been thinking of what games we can do that aren't babyish and also that the boys will join in.

We can't play totally teenage things, 'cos there is no way I am doing *Spin the Bottle* or *Slow*

Dancing with a Boy when my mum could walk in at any second! Not that there are any remotely nice boys on the horizon of my life anyway. (After you have had a crush on a mega-movie star it is very hard to be interested in any normal boys — see my last journal for the *Celeb-tastic* goss!)

Anyway, I won't have time to notice boys, 'cos I'll be far too busy topping up people's glasses and doing directing to the toilet and generally making sure everyone is having the maximum fun possible. Oh, I know, maybe we could do charades and some team games of, like, *Passing the Orange Under your Chin*. We could get the Twister out too, I suppose, but somehow it is never as much fun as you think it will be and also it sometimes leads to embarrassing botty burps!

To make sure the Surprise Birthday Party is an *absolute* and *complete* surprise for Tilda, I have made up a good excuse for asking her over, which is telling her that I want my flowery scarf back. I did in fact give it to her ages ago, when I first did a makeover on her, but I'm going to pretend it was only a borrow (genius, huh?!). Then when she gets here she will discover the party and be completely *over the hills and far away* with happiness.

I haven't told Tilda's dad about the party because he might not allow it (although Mum sort of assumed I have in fact told him and I haven't quite got round to mentioning to her that I haven't, so *ssshhhhhh!!*). I'm just so scared that if I ask for his permission straight out, he'll say no, especially after he had to rescue Tilda from a teenagers' party quite recently (my fault!). Of course, *this* party will be nothing whatsoever like *that* party, but he might not realize that and anyway, seeing as how stricty he is just in general, it's much better to wait till the night. Then, once he sees all the effort we've made and how safe and supervised the party is he'll definitely let Tilda stay. The only vital thing is that after the party has started I will have to make sure Mum keeps him safely in the kitchen having coffee with her and Gloria (her friend who is helping out) and doesn't let him into the living room, where the fun is happening.

I have to go and get ready now, 'cos I need all of the 53 minutes I've got left to do my hair and make-up and that. I'm wearing this cool top I recently bought from New Look and my best jeans, but with my Special Occasion high heels instead of trainers so that I look about 17-ish years old. I am doing my hair up in the way it was at the photo shoot for the last picture, but with a few bits hanging down to soften it.

Plus, I am putting body glitter on my arms for extra sparkliness and when Jules comes I am lending it to her (and Tilda too, when she gets here – 'cos being **BFF** we all *have* to have the same!). I *soooooo* wish I could have bought that glammy hourglass dress from Girlsworld to wear tonight, but it is way too expensive to even **THINK** about.

Erk! I'm suddenly really nervous – I hope it all goes okay!

Oh, yikes! That is the doorbell and I haven't even got changed yet!

_Just writing this
quickly in the loo,_
touching up my make-up
before the Big Surprise!

Oh dear, this really weird thing just happened with
Simon Driscott, who was the person at the door.
I let him in and instead of the normal mumbling
and looking at the floor boys do as a "hello",
he did kissing me on both cheeks (yurgh!).
He looked completely _under the stars_
with excitement

My most recent made-up phrase
meaning "over the moon"!

and said he was really, really looking forward to
tonight and especially to spending it with me.

I was thinking, "Eh?" because of course he will
be spending it with me (and everyone else!), but
I had to get back upstairs and do my make-up so
I just went, "Okay, cool," and left him to set up

100

his mobile disco in the party room.

Soon everyone else was arriving and Alex was letting them in and taking coats (but only because I paid him two tubes of fruit pastilles to be the doorman – do **NOT** think he is naturally polite or anything!).

Mum was a bit grumpy about there being more than 10 guests and she told me that if **ANYTHING** gets broken or spilled then it is coming out of my pocket money – *GULP!* – so I really hope everyone behaves!

When I was chatting to people and pouring out fruit cocktails, Simon Driscott came up and **PUT HIS ARM ROUND ME!** (Weird or what?!) I thought it was one of his strange jokes, like when he points a banana from his lunchbox at me and goes, *Use the Force, Lucy!* so I wriggled away, going, "I *soooooo* do not get your sense of humour, Simon. You're acting like my *date*, but I have no idea why that is funny. Is it off *Star Trek* or something?"

Simon looked at me all confusedly and then he said really fumingly, "But I...you...we... This is intolerable, Lucy. In fact, I'm storming out of here right now!"

And while I was still standing there thinking "*Eh?*" he stormed out of the party room and slammed the door. Everyone was staring then, also thinking "*Eh?*".

Then Simon Driscott stormed back *in*, looking all red and flustery, and said, "I will be storming out shortly, but first I have to pack up my mobile disco!"

I was panicking then, completely not knowing what I'd said wrong and going, "Why are you so upset? I don't get it! And also, don't take the mobile disco or there'll be no party!"

Simon Driscott did one of his *snort of derision* thingies and growled, "That's all you're really interested in, isn't it?"

I went, "No, but…"

That's when he determinedly started

dismantling the mobile disco. It was just *soooooo* awful and the slowest storming-out I have ever seen. I just stood there watching, having no idea of how to fix things, because how can you make something right when you don't even know what you've done wrong?

Luckily Jules persuaded him to stay and do the music 'cos the party is for *Tilda* not *me*, and it wouldn't be fair on her, but Simon Driscott is still not even looking me in the eye. *Grrr!* Boys are so moody and temperamental and I will never fully get them!

Anyway, everyone is here now, so I have to forget about that and make the trick phone call to Tilda. I'm *soooooo* excited! I can't wait to see the look on her face when I open that door!!!!!!

Sunday morning, about 11 a.m.

I finally fell asleep about 5 a.m., I think. Mum has let me stay in bed and she's even brought me breakfast on a tray, so things must be really awful!

You know I said my worst nightmare about the party was the boys not dancing? Well, something way worse has happened, because there was in fact NO PARTY.

Well, no, I mean, there was a party but... oh.

I'm not explaining it very well, 'cos I'm so massively upset.

There *was* a Surprise Birthday Party, but there was no birthday girl.

Well, there was a birthday girl but only for about 5-ish minutes or probably less.

And she was very surprised...

Just not very happy.

At all.

Oh, I can hardly stand to write this down –
everything has gone utterly, completely and
horribly wrong! I'm honestly not sure if Tilda will
ever speak to me again – and it's *soooooo* not
fair!

It seems strange now to think how completely
excited we were about the party, but of course we
didn't know then the awfulness of what was going
to happen.

Right, I am going to say it now.

You know I was going back downstairs to make
the call to Tilda? Well, I did, and I said about
needing the hippy scarf back right this minute.
She said they were just having their tea, but I said
I must have it very urgently and she would have to
bring it straight round. All the time I had to sound
serious and not start laughing 'cos it would have
ruined the surprise. But now I realize I should

have just told her the truth about the party after all.

"But I thought you gave that scarf to me?" she almost whispered.

"Oh, no, it was only a borrow," I said. "And I need it for something very important right this actual second."

"Fine. I'll get Dad to drive me round now," said Tilda in a very cold voice. "And by the way, thanks for saying 'Happy Birthday'!" and then she slammed the phone down.

I was so excited about the party I didn't notice exactly how upset she was, plus I thought she would turn all joyful when we showed her the party and the whole scarf thing wouldn't matter.

But I was **MASSIVELY** wrong.

About ten minutes later we heard Tilda's dad's car pull up, and we turned out all the lights in the living room, and everyone hid. There was loads of whispering and giggling and people going *shussshhh!!!!* When they were finally quiet (I put Jules in charge of *keeping* them quiet!) I shut the

living-room door. And I was so excited because
I thought the moment of surprise we'd worked so
hard for was just about to come!!!

I went down the hall and opened the front
door. My plan was to invite Tilda in, and then
throw open the living-room door and Simon
would turn the disco lights on and everyone would
shout, "Surprise!"

But when I opened the door Tilda threw the
scarf at me and burst into tears, and blurted out all
this terrible stuff, like, "How could you do this to
me, Lucy? I know you and Jules avoided talking
about my birthday because you don't want to do
anything with me, and I know you arranged the
photo shoot for the afternoon I had piano practice
so I couldn't be part of it! And I know you two
have been whispering about me and e-mailing and
passing notes behind my back! I know you don't
want to be friends with me any more, but why
couldn't you just have the guts to say so, instead of
leaving me out and going off together! Well, now I

know what sort of person you really are, Lucy Jessica Hartley, and I never want to see you or that Julietta Garcia Perez Benedicionatorio ever again!"

And with that she stormed off back to the car. I should have stopped her, but I was in too much *shocked stunnedness* to say anything. I just couldn't believe what was happening. By the time I managed to go, "No, Tilda, wait!" the car was screeching away from the curb. Tilda just gave me such a horrible look through the window, worse than anyone has ever given me in my entire life. My stomach lurched and jolted and I felt like I was going to be instantly sick, so I lunged into the downstairs loo and leaned over the sink but nothing came out. Then I sat on the closed seat of the toilet and just STARED at the wall.

I just didn't know what to do. Everyone was in there, waiting for a party, and the birthday girl had gone home crying. Worse, she thought I'd been a horrible moo to her, which I would *never* be! It was all so mixed up and unfair and awful that I just started having a massive cry my actual self.

That's when Mum came and found me, and I fell into hugging her, sobbing like mad. My mascara had probably run, and I was all snotty, and people from the party (including Jules) were coming into the hall to find out what was happening and seeing the total mess I looked like, but I didn't care one bit. All I cared about was Tilda. Through sniffling gulps I managed to explain to Mum and Jules what had happened.

"But why didn't Mr. Van der Zwan just explain it to her?" Mum asked.

"Erm," I went, feeling my stomach sink even further into my shoes.

"Lucy?" said Mum.

"Erm, well, I didn't exactly tell him about the party," I mumbled. "I just thought—"

"Lucy!" Mum cried. "You told me you had!"

"But I didn't, not in exact words," I muttered, hardly even daring to look at her. "You just kind of assumed..."

"Honestly!" Mum sighed. "It's not on to lie to me, Lucy. And before you argue, lying by omission is lying all the same."

I wasn't *going* to argue – because I knew she was right. "I just really wanted to make sure Tilda could have the party and I thought maybe Mr. Van der Zwan—"

"Wouldn't have let her?" said Mum, finishing for me. "But just think how she must be feeling now!"

"I know!" I groaned, and burst into fresh sobs just by thinking about it. "I'm so sorry."

Mum took a deep breath and gave me a hug. "Well, it's too late now. I think you've got the point, Lu. Right, let's just deal with things from here, shall we? We'll wait for them to get home and then call up and explain," she said softly. "The party will probably be back on in half an hour. Meanwhile, Jules, can you make sure everyone has a drink and knows what's happening?"

Jules was just staring into space looking really

shaken. "Jules?" said Mum again, putting her arm round us both. I realized then that Jules was just as upset as me. After all, Tilda probably hates her just as much. "Yeah, sure," said Jules and she wandered back into the living room in a daze.

I wish I could tell you that the party was all back on within half an hour and everything was all right again, but the terrible truth is that it wasn't.

I rang Tilda's house, but as soon as I said who it was, Mr. Van der Zwan growled, "I think you're the last person Tilda wants to speak to right now, young lady!" and slammed the phone down.

That made me so upset that Mum got this determined look on her face and rang back. "Mr. Van der Zwan," she said, before he could even start talking, "you have to listen. There's been a terrible mistake!"

"The only mistake there's been is that I allowed Matilda-Jane to play with your daughter all this time!" he shouted. When Mum saw me hearing what he'd said, she clamped the phone really hard onto her ear, but by how red and flustery she went I knew he was saying even more awful things. That absolutely made my stomach sink into my shoes and I started crying again.

"Mr. Van der Zwan, I really think…" Mum began, but then the line went dead. She held the phone away from her and frowned at it. "Well, I'm afraid he's not going to listen to anything we have to say tonight. He's far too angry. Oh, Lu, I just wish you'd told him…" She stopped herself. "But it's too late for that now." She pulled me into a hug again. "I'm afraid there's not going to be a party tonight, unless you want to carry on without Tilda?"

I shook my head. A party was the last thing I felt like. Mum said I should go and explain what had happened to my guests in the living room, but I just couldn't face them. In fact, I don't know how I'll ever face them again. Instead I burst out sobbing again and ran upstairs and buried my head right under the duvet and cried and cried. I tried not to listen to the sounds downstairs of cars pulling up and Mum explaining to parents what had happened and the front door opening and shutting loads of times. Jules came up to try and talk to me but I couldn't even face *her*.

"I can't believe this, Jules," I said, still hiding my head under the duvet. "I think Tilda really hates us. We should have realized that our secret party-planning would look like going off!"

Jules sighed and just whispered, "I know."

Mum called up the stairs that Jules's dad was here, and Jules went then, and I stayed awake the whole night and didn't sleep one single wink 'cos of all the awfulness spinning round in my head.

Well, I think Tilda and her dad must have gone out somewhere, 'cos I've been ringing and ringing their phone all day and no one's picked it up (or they are deliberately not answering, which is way worse – the thought of that makes my stomach flip over and over like a pancake). Jules has been trying all day too, but no luck. I have just been having a sleep, 'cos of lying awake all night, and now I feel all weird and mudgy and absolutely more desperate to sort things out with Tilda than ever.

Oh, wait, I have just thought of something. I could write to Tilda and give her the letter at school tomorrow. If I do an *Ask Tilda* letter she will *have* to read it, 'cos she said she hates leaving people without any help – and that must even include me. Once she reads it she will hopefully understand that me and Jules were not going off, and everything should be okay again. But, urgh, what if she doesn't believe me? I know, I will also put some *Scientific Evidence* in with the letter to prove that we were honestly having a party for her. But what if she *still* doesn't believe me? She is usually very good at science but right now she is *soooooo* upset and she thinks I am *such* a horribly bad person that maybe she will just simply hate me forever instead. But I have to try — it is my *Last Hope*.

Be back in a min...

A min later

Right, okay, I have now got a big envelope from Mum and some *Scientific Evidence* of the party to put in it, which is:

The birthday card that I made her (this is just a mini-sized one I made for practice)

A Frazzle and Wotsit skewer canapé (I was going to send her a surprise-parcel one, but Mum said ham shouldn't be left out of the fridge for that long and I might end up poisoning her, which would definitely not demonstrate my BFFness!)

The flowery scarf which I did actually give her

Some of the silver streamery decoration thingies

Tilda's birthday present, still wrapped up

And I have copied out my letter in here so you can see what I've put.

Dear Ask Tilda,

I have a really bad problem that I hope you can help me with solving. What happened was, me and one of my **BFF** planned a Surprise Birthday Party for our other **BFF**, who was becoming 13. But we got carried away with our planning and didn't realize that to our other **BFF** it looked like we were going off together. Then when she came to the party, disaster struck because we had been so good at making it secret she didn't even realize there **WAS** a party and just thought I wanted a scarf back. I had in fact given her the scarf for keeps and it was just an excuse I made up for her to come over, but she thought I was being horrible to her (which I would never be, cross my heart and hope to ~~die~~ get so knotted up while playing Twister that it takes three really painful operations to

· sorry · ❀ · sorry · ❀ · sorry · ❀ · sorry · ❀

untangle me, and even then one foot still faces out to the side). In case my **BFF** still doesn't believe me, I am also enclosing some *Scientific Evidence* to prove the existingness of the Surprise Birthday Party.

Now I am just in the *Eternal Woe* of not knowing if my **BFF** will forgive me (if she even still *is* my **BFF** and not my former ex-**BFF**?).

Only you can help me, Ask Tilda!

From

Anon xxx

PS My other **BFF** is also wallowing in sadness and is also desp to be forgiven, **BTW**!

· sorry · ❀ · sorry · ❀ · sorry · ❀ · sorry · ❀

I really, really hope that makes Tilda see the truth. I would go round and post it through her door right now, but the package is quite big and squishing it through would probably destroy the

Scientific Evidence, so I will have to wait and
give it to her at school tomorrow.

Urgh! I feel sick just *thinking* of school
tomorrow, 'cos everyone will be talking about
me having a full-scale, Mum-hugging sob-fest
on Saturday (complete with cringe-making runny
nose!) and then hiding in my room while they
all got sent home with no party. How completely
embarrassing! I wish I never had to see any of
them again in my whole life ever! But I have to
go and *face the music*, 'cos I'm desp to make
up with Tilda and also, me and Simon have to
finish putting the fashion pages together or we will
miss the Monday deadline, and there will be just a
blank space in the mag, which would let everyone
down, and I am way too *professionalistic* to let
that happen.

Oh, I'm getting hungry now – I'll go and have
some of that leftover party food, even though it
reminds me of the awfulness of yesterday.

Monday lunchtime,
all alone in an endless
ocean of miserability.

I am hiding in the science room writing this, with safety goggles on for a disguise, because Jules is at lunchtime drama club and it seems like no one else in the whole school is talking to me (although I can tell that they are all talking *about* me, because there is lots of whispering that suddenly stops when I go near people).

I have also not been able to make up with Tilda, because she isn't even at school today. That's so weird, because she never has a single day off ever, so I'm sure it's to do with her still being upset about me and Jules going off. ↰

> Which we were NOT, but that's
> what she thinks!

Oh well, I will just have to go round her house after school and risk squishing the parcel through her letterbox after all.

120

Another terrible thing is the fact that Simon Driscott is in fact still **NOT** talking to me. I should be working with him on the mag **RIGHT NOW**, but when I got to the computer room at lunch he said he wouldn't let me use the fashion-shoot photos or help me with the computer bits of the designing. I was in total **FLABBERGASTED GOBSMACKEDNESS** wondering what I could possibly have done on Saturday night that has made him stay this upset. I was just trying to persuade him to do the pages with me when Mr. Wright came in and Simon said to him, "Unfortunately, Sir, the photos for the fashion shoot were somehow completely wiped from my camera before I downloaded them, so we won't be able to do Lucy's fashion feature."

I just gaped at him, wondering if he had been taken over by *Evil Forces* in the night 'cos normally he is Mr. Honest, so how could he tell such a massivo lie?!

Mr. Wright looked really upset for us, and also

stressed out, and then he took a deep breath and said, "Time is running out, kids. Unless you can get those pages done by first break tomorrow they won't be included. You'll just have to think of something else to write about, and quickly."

I didn't think disaster could strike any more than that, but this must be my most unluckiest day ever, because right then Mr. Cain strolled in and went, "Think of something else for *what*, Mr. Wright?"

Mr. Wright explained, and Mr. Cain's massive bushy single eyebrow lifted up and he gave me a snaky smile, and said, "Well, I'm sure Lucy and I can sort it out between us."

Oh, I can hardly stand to tell you what happened next. It was Mr. Cain's perfect revenge on me for being his arch nemesis, i.e. the Tambridge High fashion guru, when he is the *School Uniform Police*.

He made me put my uniform on properly straight on both shoulders and do my tie as a kipper and wash off my lipgloss and eyeliner and slap my hair back into a swot-tastic plait and then he got the school camera from the secretaries' office and – urgh, I am really having to **MAKE** myself write this 'cos I *sooooo* don't want to. Well, basically he is making me be the model in his feature called *"Acceptable Standards of School Uniform – A Pull-Out and Keep Easy Reference Guide for Pupils"*, which he is going to write this afternoon. So he took pictures of me looking completely gross-o-matic, like this:

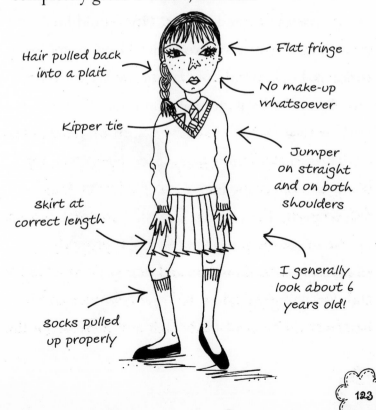

Hair pulled back into a plait

Flat fringe

No make-up whatsoever

Kipper tie

Jumper on straight and on both shoulders

Skirt at correct length

I generally look about 6 years old!

Socks pulled up properly

Now my reputation as *Style Queen* of the school will be destroyed forever, and everyone will think I *wanted* to do this feature with Mr. Cain because I massively love our *gross-o-matic* sludge-green uniform, and then everyone will also think I'm totally from the Kingdom of Nerdonia and my life will be ruined for all time. I can't believe that all the hard work we did on the fashion pages has been completely ruined – and all because of Simon Driscott! How could he be so horrible after we worked so hard on the shoot and the designs and layouts and that? What have I possibly done to make him this annoyed with me?

This is most truly the worst day of my life. Oh, hang on, I have to go and empty out my safety goggles, because they are filling up with tears.

I am writing this sitting on Tilda's front step,

still in limitless torrents of woefulness.

Well, I walked all the way over here after school, and I have rung the doorbell loads of times, but no one is answering, so I squashed my parcel through the letterbox in the end. I have also shouted through it, going, "Tilda, I've written you a letter and I'm going to stay sitting out here till you read it, even if it takes forever, so there!"

Well that was half an hour ago and I am getting really cold. What if I really do have to sit here forever and then I wither away from lack of dinner?

Jules was coming as well, to *face the music* with me, but her mum rang her mobile after school and asked her to go and collect Benito and Benita from Junior Karate, so I am having to face it on my own.

I just now rang the bell again, really hard and for ages and ages, and yelled, "Please, Tilda, don't let me starve out here alone!" but still no one has come. I should have saved my apple instead of eating it at last break.

Oh, hang on, the door is openi

Later,
at home, after dinner.

I am right now meant to be doing my science homework, which is something to do with electro-magnetic polar current forces that I just entirely did not get, but I am writing this instead 'cos I just **HAVE** to tell you what happened when Tilda's door opened.

Well, Tilda stood there (not Mr. V der Z, luckily!) holding my *Ask Tilda* letter, which was all covered in Frazzle and Wotsit powder and ripped where the cocktail stick had stabbed into it. She was all in teariness, and she was going, "Is this really true?"

"Yes, of course," I promised.

Tilda came and sat down on the step next to me. "Oh, Lucy, I'm so sorry, I just feel so stupid!" she cried. "And sorry about my dad too – I'll explain everything to him. I should have trusted

127

you and Jules that you'd never go off, but I've been under such pressure with *Ask Tilda*, and…" Her voice went really crackly then, and it was like she could hardly speak, so I put my arm round her. "And I always think about my mum a lot around my birthday," she added, in almost a whisper.

I felt completely awful then, and my stomach was churning like it does sometimes after I've had leftover curry round Dad's. "I'm sorry," I blurted out. "I should have realized you'd be missing your mum on your birthday. How could I have ever thought you'd want a *party*! It's **MY** fault."

"No, really, it was so nice of you to do the party," Tilda sniffled. "It probably would have cheered me up, if I hadn't jumped to conclusions and spoiled it all! It's all **MY** fault!"

"No, it's **MY** fault," I insisted. "I can see now how me and Jules gave you the wrong idea and made you think we were going off."

"No, it's **MY** fault," Tilda insisted, even more insistingly than me. "I should have told you how I was feeling before!"

"But it's MY fault for not telling your dad about the party," I insisted, most insistingly.

"No, it's MY fault for having a stricty dad!" cried Tilda.

That was when we looked at each other and burst out laughing at our own complete idio-city. When I got my breath back I went, "Maybe it's just an unfortunate case of crossed wires."

"True," said Tilda. "But the wires wouldn't have got crossed if I'd told you and Jules how left out I was feeling, instead of just bottling it up and then exploding like...erm..."

"A fruit smoothie in the sun?" I suggested.

"Exactly," said Tilda. Then she groaned. "Oh no, what must everyone think, who came to the party! They must all hate me for jumping to conclusions and being horrid to you! There's no way I can go into school tomorrow!

In fact, I'll have to keep coming up with fake lurgies forever!"

"No one hates you," I promised her. "It's me who should be changing schools, or moving countries, more like! Mum had to send everyone home after you went 'cos I was so upset, so there *was* no party! Plus, everyone saw me having a snot-full blaaah-fest, and if there is a single person in the school who hasn't heard about that, which I highly doubt, and who still thinks I'm a *Stand-up Babe*, well, they won't when Mr. Cain's feature comes out!"

Tilda looked confused and I had to explain to her all about how Simon won't work with me on the mag, and how I don't know why, and how weird he was when we were setting up before the party, like putting his arm round me as a *Star Trek* joke, then getting in a total dark and stormy for no reason when I told him I didn't get why it was funny.

Tilda got this strange knowing sort of look on her face, like she does when she's solving hard algebra for her homework, and said, "I think I can sort that out for you."

"Wow! How?" I asked, rhyming with excitement.

Tilda smiled all mysteriously. "Well, I can't promise anything, but let's just say it may be another case of crossed wires."

I didn't get what she meant, but I'm glad she's going to try and fix things with Simon for me. Even if it's too late for the mag, maybe she could stop him actually hating me, which feels totally horrible. "So does that mean you'll come to school tomorrow after all?" I asked.

"I'll have to, won't I?" Tilda sighed. "If I want to save you from the eternal embarrassment of being Mr. Cain's model super-swot!"

"Urgh! Don't even mention it!" I said grumpily. "I can hardly stand to even **THINK** about it!"

"I promise I will do my absolute best to get your fashion pages back in the mag," she said all seriously.

To cheer us up, I got Tilda to unwrap her birthday present from me and now she is convinced that I have actual psychic powers 'cos her dad got her an actual mobile!! Tilda loved the prezzie and went and got her new phone and put it on straight away. Then I put her new number in my address book and we rang each other even though we were sitting right next to each other. Tilda told me on the phone how she had a nice day with her dad on her birthday (before the party upset of course) going to the cinema and being allowed a big-sized thing of Coke and then visiting her grandparents.

Then we rang Jules. I listened in while they did the **MY FAULT**, no it was **MY FAULT** thing that me and Tilda had done and then I joined in with them doing the "Make friends, make friends" song we always do after any of life's adversity. Oh, it is such a relief for us all three to be **BFF** again, but really **TRAGIC** that Tilda missed out on having her party. I just feel 100% awful about that, even if it was only 57% my fault. Okay, more like 81%.

Anyway, Tilda went in and explained to her dad what had happened, and then I was thinking *GULP!* 'cos Mr. Van der Zwan came out, but luckily he just said how sorry he was and gave me a lift home. He stopped off at a posh florist on the way and got a *ginormous* bouquet of flowers which turned out to be for Mum, to say sorry for the awful things he said on the phone. Mum did her hands-on-her-hips/pursed-lips thing and didn't take the flowers at first, but then when Mr. V der Z had done enough grovelling she did and she also invited him in for a coffee. That was cool 'cos me and Tilda went in the living room and texted each other while watching a *Friends* repeat on E4.

Well, time to tackle the electro-central magnetic forces homework. I'll go downstairs and see if Mum has a clue what it's on about.

And fingers crossed for me for tomorrow!

In the loos at lunchtime,
feeling totally fabulastically amazing!!!!!!

I just had to write this straight away to tell you that Tilda completely fixed things between me and Simon Driscott – *YAY!* – though I utterly do not get *how* she did it! Do you ever get the feeling that when three people are having a talk sometimes two of the people are having a different talk at the same time, and the third person (i.e. me) doesn't have a clue what they're on about? Well that's how I felt. But anyway, I will write down the exact things they said, and maybe you can work it out.

Tilda: Simon, I know you're only upset with Lucy because she didn't get your *Star Trek* joke, in which you were demonstrating being a Cling On (Klingon? Kerlingon?) by putting your arm round her, and that it's nothing to do with you fancying her and thinking that you were invited to the party as her date. If that was true, which it's not, but if it was, it would not be Lucy's fault you got the wrong end of the stick about her feelings. So it would not be fair to take your disappointment out on her.

Simon Driscott: I know but... Ahem, I mean, it was entirely her non-appreciation of my *Cling On* joke that raised my hackles.

— Klingion? Oh, whatever   — His whats?

Tilda (to me): Lucy, please apologize to Simon for not understanding his joke.

Me: Er, sorry.

Tilda (to Simon): Simon, please accept Lucy's apology.

Simon Driscott: Fine.

Tilda: Well, in that case, now we've cleared everything up, there's nothing to stop you two working together to finish the fashion pages, is there?

Simon Driscott: Well, erm…

Tilda: Because you wouldn't want anyone, or, for example, *everyone* to think there is any other reason that you were in a mood with Lucy, would you, Simon?

Simon Driscott (looking startled and scared like a rabbit caught in the headlights, as my mum calls it): Definitely not! Not that there *is*, erm, any other reason.

Tilda (smiling): No, of course not. Right, you'd better get cracking then.

So while I was just standing there thinking, "*Eh?*" Simon Driscott turned round to me and went, "Right then, Lucy, if Mr. Wright lets us off English and we work through break, we'll just about have our pages ready for when the magazine goes to the printers."

"Oh, Simon, thank you!" I cried. "I'm so glad we got that silly joke thing cleared up!" I was just *sooooo* full of joyfulness that I threw my arms round him in a big hug without even thinking that he is a boy. He went all red with total embarrassment then and gabbled, "Right well, no time to lose with pointless hugging, especially as we are just sort of friends with no fancying going on whatsoever."

And I gave Tilda a big hug of thanks and off we went to explain to Mr. Wright that the photos had amazingly reappeared. I shouted, "It's a miracle!" for extra believableness, and luckily he let us get straight on with our pages – *phew!*

The glitter-ball background worked brilliantly, and the copy looked really good. We already knew roughly what pictures we were using and the colours and that, so it didn't take too long to put it all together (and we found some really cool fonts too!).

The finished pages looked fab and when Mr. Wright came to check on us at the end of break he was really happy with them too.

"I'm just so relieved it's going in the mag and not Mr. Cain's feature," I blurted out. "So now my life isn't ruined forever after all!" Then I had a sudden realization of how angry Mr. Cain would be when he found out. "Oh, but who's going to tell him?" I stammered.

"Let's not mention the changes to him just yet, shall we?" said Mr. Wright, with a wink. "I wouldn't want him interfering when what you've done is so wonderful."

So we agreed that it was best to keep *silencio*.

When Mr. Wright had gone I said to Simon Driscott, "Ha! So *he* finds Mr. Cain as annoying as we do, but of course he can't say so straight out 'cos of his professionality."

"You mean, professionalism," said Simon.

"Oh, go and *spontaneously combust*," I said back.

It's so nice that things are back to normal between us again. I didn't used to think it was actually possible to be sort of friends with a boy, but now I sort of think that it sort of is.

Still Tuesday

At home, lying on my bed,
not feeling quite so totally
fabulastically amazing.

Oh dear, just when I thought everything was fabby
again, it's like, *Houston, we have a major
problem*. When I got in just now Mum was
waiting all nervously to find out how things
had gone with Simon Driscott and the mag
and I started gabbling on about how brainy Tilda
mysteriously managed to sort it all out for me, and
how our fashion pages got finished, and I was just
burbling about text size and backgrounds and fonts
and captions and all that when I noticed she wasn't
looking exactly *over the moon.*

*No time to make up a new phrase 'cos
urgent work to do – as you'll see*

That's when I realized her nervosity maybe wasn't
about the mag after all.

"Mum, I know something's wrong 'cos of my *Female Intuition*," I said, and I persuaded her to tell me what it was even though she didn't want to.

"Oh, Lu," she sighed. "Unfortunately your father hasn't impressed the radio station bosses at all with his show. When we listened, I was hoping he just had some teething problems, but it seems that things haven't improved and so Robert Hyde is letting him go."

"Letting him go where?" I asked, and Mum gave me a long despairing look till I suddenly got that she meant *letting him go* as in FIRING HIM!

I went, "But that's so unfair, 'cos he's brilliant!!" But we both knew that wasn't true.

Mum reckons Robert Hyde's cross 'cos Dad won't play country and western for the L-DLDs and 'cos he isn't funny or even sometimes *awake* between records. He's only got one more week while they find someone else and then that is IT. As in *curtains*.

I suddenly felt really angry then, and I still do. "It just isn't FAIR!" I stormed. "I mean, Dad is trying his best! This could ruin his whole future!"

"It's even worse than that, Lu," Mum said quietly, then she explained how she'd been hoping his DJ job would go well so that he could pay something towards the house costs and family expenses, but that now she'll have to go full-time at work.

She's right – that *is* even worse.

I went, "But you can't go to work full-time, not

141

for that *Prehistoric Idiot* Mr. Snellerman."

We call him that because he does not understand
the needs of modern working women or how it is sexist
to call Mum "sweetheart" and tell her to make his tea
when she is just as professional as a man.

Mum looked really small and tired then,
and went, "Oh, Lu, I'm so sorry to be discussing
this with you. When your father and I split up I
promised myself I wouldn't put any of the burden
on you and Alex. But I'm just so tired of struggling
on my own."

I gave her a big hug and said, "Don't worry,
I'll make everything okay – I promise," but I have
no actual idea of *how*.

Mum laughed and squeezed me tight. "That's
sweet, Lu. But unless you've got a magic wand..."

"No, but I have got a magic Teen Witch Kit,"
I told her.

And I am going to look in it for Dad-career-
saving spells right now.

Well, sadly there is nothing in my Teen Witch Kit
about *Making Awful DJs into Good Ones*.
I also looked up *Helping Dads* and *How to Stay
Awake All Night When You've Already Tried
Coffee*, but there was zilchio.

Luckily all is not lost 'cos I have just now
called on something even more
powerful than witchcraft.
Yes, I mean **BFF** Power.
I have in fact called on
Jules and Tilda (by the
power of mobie-phones!)
to have an emergency meeting in the little
doorway round the back of the art room
tomorrow before school and help me solve the
Dad crisis. I'm sure with all of our thinking caps
on we can come up with a Dad-saving solution,
can't we?

Wednesday morning,

in the little doorway round
the back of the art room.

Jules and Tilda have just headed into the school
'cos the first bell has gone, but I'm staying here to
quickly write this. I just *have* to tell you that I was
right, my plan to use **BFF** Power totally worked! Me
and Jules walked in early and met Tilda here at 8.15
a.m. And then we got straight on with our thinking.

Tilda said, "Why don't we take the scientific
approach and look at all the variables. Then we can
see where there is room to man~~œuv~~er man~~œ~~ver
man~~œu~~vre." *Can't spell that word, but hopefully
you get what I mean*

And I went, "Good thinking", like I totally
did get what she meant instead of feeling vaguely
confused.

So Tilda wrote down the *variables*, which
apparently are:

144

1) Time of show

2) Content of show

3) Demographic of audience

 Meaning: who listens to it

Well, I told her that number 1 is completely fixed and unnegotiable. The Graveyard Shift is the worst slot you can actually *get,* and Dad is in most dangerous danger of losing even *that*, so there's no way Robert Hyde would suddenly give him a better one.

Plus, I said that number 2 is also non-variable 'cos Dad would rather **DIE** than play the country music that **L-DLD**s like. Then I suddenly blushed bright red 'cos I'd said Dad would rather *die*, which is only a phrase, but Tilda's mum *has* actually died, and I felt really awful and embarrassed and clapped my hand over my mouth.

Luckily Tilda said, "Oh, Lu, don't look like that! I know you didn't mean it literally! You don't have to walk on eggshells around me."

I said *okay*, but secretly I am going to try hard to stop saying phrases like that.

So it absolutely had to be number 3, *Who listens to it*, that we could ~~ma.uver~~ ~~man.evre~~ manoeuvre. *Oh, hang on, I think maybe that is right!*

"So you mean we have to think of another group of people who are up in the middle of the night apart from L-DLDs," said Jules.

"Exactly," said Tilda.

We all had a hard think and I handed round some Babybels to keep our strength up, but no inspiration struck. Then my mind was wandering off and I was thinking this thing that had nothing to do with the problem, and then I was thinking, *Why am I thinking of this thing that has nothing to do with the problem when I am in fact meant to be thinking about the problem?* Then I suddenly realized that the thing I was thinking about that I thought I shouldn't be thinking about was in fact the **SOLUTION** to the problem!!!

"Students!" I blurted out, making Jules and Tilda stare at me confusedly.

I explained about the thing I had been thinking, which was about ages and ages ago when I had a *hsʊrc terces* on Jules's big bro JJ and I had to think of a way of getting close to him on the walk home from the school disco. What happened was, I told him that students had pinched all the traffic cones and manhole lights to put on their pinched shopping trolleys to make transport for pub crawls, so we should link arms or there might be a danger of falling down an unlit manhole. And that made me realize how students are always up really late 'cos they only have about one lecture a week or something, which is like maybe as long as a double lesson, so they get to have a lie-in every day, and I also said how they like rock music and comedy and that.

"They could be your dad's audience!" cried Jules.

"He could aim his whole show at them," added Tilda. "Brilliant thinking, Lu!"

Cool or what?!

So we scoffed some more Babybels and did some more thinking and came up with:

The Radio Rescue Plan
Da-daaaaa!

Our brainwave is that Dad puts on a funny show for students called *Brian's Midnight Feast* (Tilda made up the cool name) where he holds weird and wacky phone-ins and plays silly and also cheesy songs (as well as cool rock, of course!). The special show features we have thought of are:

1) The Cheese Feast
This is where students ring in with the cheesiest love songs they can think of. Dad decides which is the most cheesy and plays it, and the winner gets a free cheeseburger at the Cool Cats café (we just have to arrange it with Reggie!).

2) Things That Go Bump in the Night

This is where Dad drops an object on the floor and the student who's playing the game can ask 5 questions about it to try and guess what it is. If they get it right, they win 2 tickets to the town's Ghost Tour!

3) Brian's Midnight Munchies

Students call in and tell Dad what they have in their cupboards and he comes up with a fab (and probably gross!!!) recipe they can make right that second.

My brain seemed to be having so many ideas that I suddenly blurted out another one, which was nothing to do with Dad's show. The idea was to have Tilda's birthday party again, because it's so totally unfair that she didn't get her last one. Plus, when everyone goes home after the party, we could have a sleepover with just us three there to listen to Dad's new radio show! How totally fab is that?!

Tilda said, "But I couldn't have another Surprise Birthday Party, could I? For a start it's not my birthday any more and secondly it's not a surprise, seeing as you just told me."

"But we can change it to being a Not-Surprising Non-Birthday Party," I cried. "And it'll be much better this time, 'cos we'll all organize it together, and get ready together and have loads of fun!"

Tilda looked really excited then. "Well, I'd really love to have a party..." she began.

"That's settled then!" said Jules. "Oh, it's going to be *soooooo* fab!"

And we all had a big **BFF** hug.

Oh, that's the second bell, I really have gotta go now or I will be in big trouble!

Byeeeeee!!!!!!

Newsflash!

As soon as I got home I told Mum about the second party idea and she said we could have it here again! So I phoned Jules and Tilda and they each asked while I waited on the phone (the suspense was too much to possibly hang up!) and they are allowed over too, so *Yippeeee!!!* Even better, Tilda's dad is insisting on paying this time, so Mum is relieved and we can probably even splash out on the glacé cherries and little umbrellas and stuff for the fruit cocktails she said no to before.

Now Mum has taken Alex to Junior Karate and for a change I decided to stay here and write this. It feels really cool being left in the house on my own, even if it is only for 15 minutes. Maybe Mum is finally getting how completely mature I am.

I am starting to feel a bit weird though, and I have just been round checking everywhere for people hiding – even in silly places like under Alex's duvet and in the laundry basket. So it was lucky I had to ring Dad, 'cos it was almost like having him actually here.

I explained about the Radio Rescue Plan and he got all enthusiastic and he reckons he's going to play the guitar in it too – which is unfortunate, 'cos he is *awful*. But I didn't want to say anything to squash his keenness, so the listeners will just have to put up with it.

Hang on, I think I'll put the TV on – oh that's better, I feel much more like normal and not scared now I've got *X Factor* on in the background. Oh, and now Mum is back – yay, I survived staying here on my own!

Thursday night

just before bed. Sorry I haven't
written much - I've been v. busy!

Today Simon Driscott helped me do this cool invite
for Tilda's new party (and **BTW** he is also doing the
music again). It meant having to go to computer
club with him at lunchtime and the Geeky Minions
all looking at me like I was an alien species, but it
was *soooooo* worth it, 'cos look at this:

The Not-Surprising Non-Birthday Party!

Dear _____

Please come and celebrate it being NOT
Tilda's birthday!

On: Saturday 21st May

From: 7 p.m.— 9.30 p.m.

At: 4 The Meadows, Barnaby Road,
Sherborne (Lucy's house again)
RSVP to Lucy or Jules (or Tilda, 'cos
she knows about this one!)

When we handed out the invites, no one mentioned the me-madly-crying incident at the first party – *phew!* – maybe they were scared of getting uninvited to this one!

Friday
I wrote this in maths and
I am just now sticking it in here.

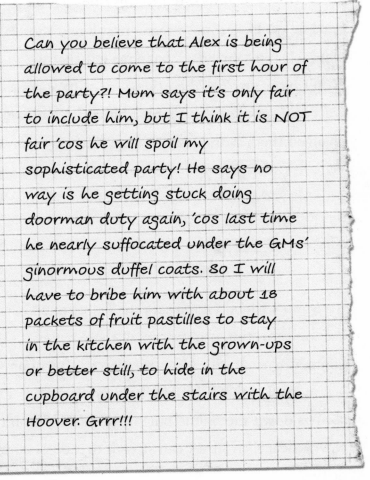

Can you believe that Alex is being
allowed to come to the first hour of
the party?! Mum says it's only fair
to include him, but I think it is NOT
fair 'cos he will spoil my
sophisticated party! He says no
way is he getting stuck doing
doorman duty again, 'cos last time
he nearly suffocated under the GMs'
ginormous duffel coats. So I will
have to bribe him with about 18
packets of fruit pastilles to stay
in the kitchen with the grown-ups
or better still, to hide in the
cupboard under the stairs with the
Hoover. Grrr!!!

Friday night

The party is only 23 hours
and 37 minutes from now!

Luckily we have some streamers still and there are
some "Happy Birthday" balloons left that we
didn't blow up, 'cos the original ones have gone all
wilty and some of them look a bit rude! We have
changed them with a marker pen, like

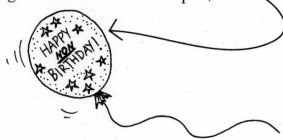

Mum's friend Gloria says she'll sort out
the food this time, so we can all three have a
pampering sesh with Mum tomorrow afternoon
– how cool is that?! I told Gloria my canapé
recipes down the phone but she just said, "Don't
worry, dear, I'm sure I can stretch to a *volervont*
or two." Huh?

Mum is also going to do our make-up, 'cos she's really good at it. She's invited Mr. Van der Zwan to stay around for the party, but she's promised to keep him in the kitchen with her and Gloria (and Alex, unless he's in the Hoover cupboard!).

Shockingly, I have still not decided what to wear. Well, I have thought of about 10 different outfits but none of them seem quite right. In my actual wildest dreams I would be wearing the fabulous 50s-style dress I borrowed for the fashion shoot, but that would be impossible as it's too expensive, and probably sold by now to one of those posh Sherborne School for Young Ladies girls we get round here. *soooooo* not fair! I have really got to pull myself together, stop dreaming about that dress and plan my outfit. After all, the party is only 23 hours and – hang on while I lean over to check my clock – 16 minutes from now!

TICK-TICK-TICK!!!

Saturday

after lunch.

I am writing this in the car, so I can keep you up-to-date minute-by-minute and actually second-by-second about the party planning. Can you believe I **STILL** haven't decided what I'm wearing tonight?! I have got *Fashion Block*, which is like *Writer's Block*, only way more serious.

Simon Driscott is doing a Fantasy Role-playing Game thingie this afternoon, so he came round early to set up his mobile disco in our house. He kept doing loud blasts of different tracks to test the sound, which was giving Mum a migraine so she suggested we go into town to The Body Shop to get our pampering stuff. That's where we're going now, right after we collect Tilda and Jules – *yippeeeeee!!!!!!*

So Gloria is supervising SD while doing the *volervonts*, which have apparently got something to do with chopped-up prawns by the looks of it.

Jules and Tilda are here now. In fact, Tilda is reading this over my shoulder 'cos the three of us are all squashed into the back seat (Mum says it makes her feel like a chauffeur when we sit like this!) and Tilda reckons it is *voluwvants*, not *volervonts*.

No, it's not that either.

Hang on, I'll get her to write it, seeing as she's such a brainy box!

Vol-au-vents

Oh, so it is three words in actual fact — how weird!

vol-au-vent

Back from town

You will not **BELIEVE** what has happened.

I mean, *really* not.

Me and Jules and Tilda were walking past Girlsworld, all linked arms, and chatting, and suddenly I stopped completely still and dragged them back and absolutely **STARED** into the shop window and

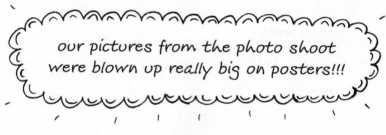

our pictures from the photo shoot were blown up really big on posters!!!

We were just in complete *shocked stunnedness*, and then it sank into us and we had a huge, squealy, jumpy-up-and-downy hug! Mum just laughed – she was in on the whole thing!

We piled into the shop and there were posters of us inside too. Cindy looked up from the box of stock she was sorting and gave us a great big grin, and so then we had lots more squealing and hugging.

After what happened before, with the party and everything, I was worried that Tilda would feel left out and so I said, "I know it's just me and Jules up there, but you are our **BFF** equally as a three."

Tilda just laughed, going, "Believe me, I'm glad it's not me in the pix, I'm far too shy! But you two look great!"

I said to Cindy, "But who – what – where – how – when?!" and she explained that Simon Driscott had e-mailed her the pix to get her approval for them to appear in the school mag and how she thought they were so good she decided to use them as advertising!

I thought that was enough amazing surprises for one day or even year or even lifetime, but Cindy had an even *more* amazing surprise for us. "Girls, I'd really like you to choose something each as payment for modelling in the photos," she said.

Wow or what?!

Mum instantly started going, "Oh, Cindy, that's

very kind, but there's really no need..." But Cindy started insisting, and then they were having that competition adults do about who can be the most polite, like "You must", "I couldn't", "But I insist", "No, $\mathcal{I}$ insist", etc., etc.

Of course, I was desperate to ask for the lovely dress that I wore at the photo shoot, which was luckily still there (and it still being there made me think it was my *destiny* to have it!), but when I looked at Mum she did an eyebrow thing which I knew meant:

Lucy Jessica Hartley, it is only polite to choose simply a pair of tights or something else small, as you well know, so stop even <u>thinking</u> about that dress!

The problem was I just couldn't tear my eyes off it. Even though I tried to make them look at these purple patterny tights that were quite nice, they just magnetically kept going back to it.

Suddenly Cindy strode across the shop and pulled the dress off the rail and put it into a bag. Mum started the politeness competition again, going, "Oh no, we can't accept—" But Cindy said, "Mrs. Hartley, I absolutely insist on Lucy having this dress, and I will not let her leave the shop without it!"

Mum sighed and said thank you, so Cindy won the politeness thing and that was that!

Cindy winked at me and handed the bag over. "No need to try it on," she said. "We know it fits!" I said a zillion thank-yous and gave her another big hug. I still absolutely cannot believe I have got **THE DRESS** and I have to keep checking in the bag to make sure it's really there.

Meanwhile Tilda helped Jules pick out a black slash-neck top with all zips on that she totally loved, and Tilda spent her birthday money from her grandparents on a fab purple silk skirt for tonight (she didn't have quite enough, but Cindy let her off the difference. She is *sooooo* cool! I *sooooo* wish she could be my aunt!).

Only 18 minutes
till party time!

Well, we have all been busy sorting out food and decorations and now everything is ready for the party. Actually, to be honest, for the last two hours we have been getting *ourselves* ready! Here are my quick pix of what we look like, all dressed up.

LUCY

JULES

TILDA

Jules and Tilda just now went to check out their new looks in the hall mirror, and I was just smoothing down my *totally fab* dress and feeling a bit (okay, a lot) nervous, when Mum suddenly gave me a big hug for no reason and went all teary. I was going, "Mum, what's wrong?" and suddenly panicking that I looked so awful I was making my own mother *cry*.

Mum shook her head and did a big sniff. "Oh, nothing," she croaked. "I'm just being silly, because, well, you look so grown-up and so beautiful."

I did a modelly pose and said, "So do you think I'm grown-up enough to have my own MAC make-up set?"

Mum laughed and went, "Nice try, kid!" then she wandered off to help Gloria with the pizzas.

So I think that's still a no, then.

It is now minus 47 minutes

till the party, 'cos it
has already started!

Just had to lock myself in the downstairs loo
and tell you that it's going *soooooo* well!
Gloria and Mum are teaching Mr. Van der Zwan
the Macarena, which is **NOT** staying in the
kitchen like they promised, but is actually
really funny!

Everyone **LOVES** the food (every single vol-
au-vent thing has been wolfed already!) and
Simon's mix of cool rock and fun party tracks
have really got the dancing going. Hmm – maybe
he's not so geeky after all!

Gotta go – Augusta Rinaldi is knocking on the
door 'cos her lot have dared her to go in the
bathroom for 2 minutes with Bill Cripps, which
means they might actually *KISS!!!*

Ooo-ooo-ohhhhhhh!!!!!!

I detect poss goss!!

Okay, okay, stop knocking!

I'll let them in now and then go and listen outside with the others – hee hee!!!

Sunday morning –
NOT v. early!

Well, Jules and Tilda are going in the shower
and getting ready and that 'cos I have said Guests
First, so I can quickly write down in here about
last night. I wanted to do it straight away after
listening to Dad do the Radio Rescue Plan
but I only just about managed to crawl upstairs
before falling fast asleep.

Well, first I **HAVE** to tell you about the 2
minutes in the bathroom thing. Some of us were
standing outside the bathroom door giggling and
straining our ears, i.e. Augusta Rinaldi's lot and
the okay boys from my class (who all had their
hair gelled back in the same style – honestly, don't
boys have *any* imagination??).

Mum came out into the hall, and I quickly
said, "Hello, lovely Mum, there is nothing
whatsoever interesting happening in the loo so

you can go back into the kitchen."

Mum did her knowing smile and said, "I wasn't born yesterday, Lu." Then she moved us aside and rapped on the door while going, "Out you come, please!" Bill Cripps and Augusta Rinaldi came out looking *soooooo* embarrassed and we all piled back into the party room after them, but they wouldn't say if they'd kissed or just listened to us listening to them.

It was really good 'cos Tilda's dad knew some games that were actually fun (I didn't think he would), like getting us to all make a circle by sitting on each other's knees and then tickling us with a feather duster to see who was first to fall over. It was *soooooo* funny when we all went down like dominoes, and I actually didn't even care that I snagged my tights!

Later on, we did singing and cutting the cake (the new one said Happy Non-Birthday Tilda!), and Tilda blew out the candles and made a wish. Because of my *Natural Curiosity* I instantly wanted to know what it was, but she wouldn't tell (she really is Miss Mysterious, sometimes!). Then she did a little speech thanking everyone for coming and the grown-ups for organizing the party stuff. Then she added, "And I would especially like to thank Lucy and Jules for all their effort, twice, and for being Stand-up Babes and the best ever Best Friends Forever a girl could ever have! And let's hope that's the end of our crossed wires!"

Everyone laughed then, and Tilda cut the cake. Mr. Van der Zwan was snapping away with his camera, and even though she's too shy to be a model, Tilda looked totally beautiful and shining with happiness – *Picture Perfect*, in fact!

Then Simon Driscott slammed on some Kaiser Chiefs and we all started moshing and Mum had a total *Lampshade Panic*. But it was good in a way because she actually begged us to do *Slow Dancing* instead!

Me and Jules had to kidnap Simon Driscott and take over on the mobile disco, 'cos he said no way was he playing "smoochy romantic nonsense". (But he didn't seem to mind when the Extended Maths girls were asking him to dance!)

I even had a dance with him as we are such a fab fashiony team, and luckily he didn't accidentally trip forward and nearly snog me with tongues this time (he explained that that is how the *Unfortunate Incident* happened at the school disco last year!).

Although I made the grown-ups go in the kitchen for the *Slow Dancing*, I could see them peeking round the corner, so there was not a lot of tonsil tennis or hands on bums. Jamie Cousins asked Tilda to dance (very brave, 'cos if there was any tonsil tennis or hands on bums whatsoever, Mr. V der Z would have made him into a boy-flavoured vol-au-vent!).

When it was time to go home no one wanted to. Mum put the main living-room light on so everyone could check they'd got all their stuff and suddenly it was like the party magic was over and we were just our normal selves standing there with some crisps squashed into the carpet and too much hair gel on (the boys!). Me and Jules and Tilda also didn't want the party to be over, but then again we sort of did, because of us having the *Radio Show Sleepover* straight after.

We helped with the clearing up and Mr. Van der Zwan gave Simon's dad a hand with loading up the mobile disco into his Volvo, and then they stood around discussing Volvos in that weird way dads do where they act like the cars are actually people.

We all gave Gloria big hugs of thanks and then Mr. Van der Zwan took her home while me, Tilda and Jules snuggled down in the living room with Mum and listened to Dad's radio show.

The great news is that it sounded really cool – I just hope it's enough to save Dad's job!

Dad had made up this fab jingle for his show that goes ♪ *"Brian's Midnight Feast!"* ♪♪ and then you hear lots of munching (he recorded that himself by eating Twixs). He played loads of cool rock and some silly songs too, like the "Hold a Chicken in the Air" one that Jules's dad sings to make Benito and Benita laugh. It was brill when he did the *Things That Go Bump in the Night* competition, you know where you drop something on the floor and play the sound back and people have to guess what it is? The student who got through to play the game was all like, "What's up, dude?" and he made it extra funny by guessing crazy things like a baby elephant and a piano, when really Dad had dropped a frying pan.

Brian's Midnight Munchies went really well too. The boy who phoned in said he had

Tin of beans

Lump of cheese

Half an onion (but he wasn't sure how long it had been in the fridge)

Dad said, "Bin the onion, dude, before it kills you – they pick up all sorts of bacteria in the fridge once they've been cut open."

Mum was completely wowed by this, going, "Gosh, so he did learn something from me during our marriage after all!"

But then Dad said the boy should pinch a slice of bread from his housemate and do cheesy beans on toast, and Mum went all tight-lipped, going, "Well, I certainly never taught him to condone stealing!"

Me, Jules and Tilda even had a midnight feast at actual midnight too, while listening to Brian's Midnight Feast – *spooky or what?!*

Then we fell asleep for ages, but we were woken up by the terrible sound of ~~cats drowning~~ whoops, I mean, Dad's guitar playing. Well, I suppose it didn't sound that bad – erm, okay, to be honest, it *did*! The best bit of all was when Dad thanked us **LIVE ON AIR** for our input. (I just hope no one thinks we told him to play the guitar!)

Tilda says this new show is great, 'cos even if Dad makes a mistake like going to sleep or eating on air, Robert Hyde will think he is doing a *Postmodern Deconstruction of the Medium* on purpose and the students will love it. I have no idea what she was on about, but it sounds cool!

Oh, my mobile just went and it was Tilda ringing me from the kitchen to say that our baked beans and bacon toasties are ready (messy, but yummy!).

Sunday the 22nd of May
at 4.52 p.m. precisely

News Update!

This is Lucy Jessica Hartley with the brill and fab news update that Dad's boss was really impressed with the radio show and he is letting Dad stay!!! Yessity-yes-yes!!!!

I know this 'cos he popped round this afternoon when Tilda and Jules had gone home and told me, Mum and Alex all about it.

"You've really come to the rescue, Lu, and your friends, of course," he said.

"No problem," I went, "there's just the small matter of our fee…"

I was joking, but he actually did give me some cash to treat me and Jules and Tilda to something nice for saving his whole career. Then he gave Alex some too so he didn't start moaning about how it wasn't fair.

I gave Dad a hug of thanks, and he did something very un-Dad-like and pulled me onto his lap for an even bigger hug. Alex came in too and then we all nearly toppled off the chair, but I didn't care.

As Dad was being un-Dad-like I decided to do something very un-Lucy-like and tell my private emotional feelings to him. "It is just so fab to have you around," I said. Then I felt a bit embarrassed with Mum and Alex listening, so I added, "Even if you are awful at guitar and you can't sing and you do embarrassing dancing down the street when people with actual eyes are watching!"

Mum and Alex laughed, and Dad went, "Charming!" but I know he didn't really mind because he just squeezed me even tighter.

It was so funny then because he spotted the flowers from Mr. Van der Zwan in a vase on the kitchen table and he instantly went all sulky, demanding to know who sent them!

Mum laughed and said, "Well, that's really not your concern, is it, Brian?" and Dad went even more huffity and grumbled, "I just think if someone's got that kind of money to burn they should give it to charity, man!"

Anyway – we have saved Dad's job – *yippeeeeee!!!* And I think I know what me and the girls can spend the thank-you money on…

Monday morning break

In the loos, hiding from
certain stricty teachers!

Sorry this is on loo roll – I forgot my journal
but I'm desp to tell you what happened this
morning. The school mags are back from the
printers and they were given out during form
time before assembly. Our fashion feature
looks totally fab, and so does Jules's Watch
It! column and the Ask Tilda page.

   In assembly, Mr. Wright did a bit of a
talk about how we put the mag together
and he said this really nice thing about
special thanks to Lucy and Simon for
submitting the fashion pages at the last
minute, despite technical difficulties, and then
we had to do clapping for everyone involved. I
glanced round at Mr. Cain and it was
obviously the first time he had heard about
the swap back to our pages – I could tell

181

that his feet were nearly boiling in his sergeant-major boots!

Mr. Cain has obviously seen the mag now though, 'cos at the start of break he was waiting outside our class, and when I came out he said, "Lucy Jessica Hartley, I would like a word with you, please, about the inappropriate clothing shown in your fashion feature." GULP! He must mean the miniskirts!

I pretended to actually need the loo really badly and ran off down the corridor and now I am hiding out in here!

Oh, I have just stuck my head round the door and he is going after Mr. Wright instead.

Yippeeeeee!

I'm freeeeee!!

Byeeeeee!!!

(Oh, that all rhymes, how cool!)

<u>At home,</u>
eating a Wagon Wheel. (At last,
I got there before Dad!)

I managed to persuade Mr. Wright to let me have
6 copies of **WORD!** for my future portfolio to take
to design interviews or for when I apply for
fashion college (if Mum doesn't nab them to show
her friends first!!).

So me and Jules and Tilda had the most
amazing day of being on *Cloud 9*, with people
thanking us for the party (Augusta Rinaldi is now
going out with Bill Cripps, **BTW**!) and saying
how cool our mag stuff is. And I can honestly tell
you that when we all linked arms and headed out
of the school gates (off to the Cool Cats café to
spend Dad's money!) I was happier than I can
ever remember being in my whole entire life. And
that is a long time – very-nearly-13 years, in
actual fact.

Oh no, this is the last page of my journal. *Boo!* *Hiss!* But don't worry, I will buy a new one with the change from our smoothies (and Jules's cheese sandwich, of course) and write again soon.

Love ya, girls!

Lucy Jessica Hartley...
xxx
♡

My cool talent quiz is on
the next page, BTW.

Lucy Jessica Hartley's Talent Quiz

Which job would you bag on the school magazine team? Find out with my fab quiz!

1) Your mates ask your advice on:

A) What to be seen in, where to be seen in it, and who to be seen in it with!

B) Their problems, parents, friendships, anything – you're a great listener.

C) Interesting things to do or fun ideas for parties.

2) Where are you in the group pix with your mates?

A) Right in the centre, telling everyone how to pose for the best shots!

B) Somewhere at the edge, watching how everyone acts.

C) Invisible! ('Cos you're always the one holding the camera!)

3) Which of the images below is your favourite?

A)   B)   C)

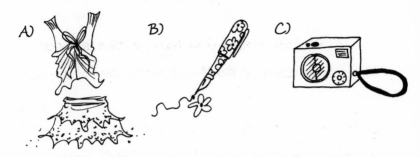

4) You're shooting a fab fashion feature and this utterly untrendy boy keeps getting his lopsided haircut and kipper tie in the way. Do you:

A) Escort him off the premises immediately!

B) Talk to him – there could be an interesting person underneath that strange get-up.

C) Work him into the shot as a contrast to the groovy models.

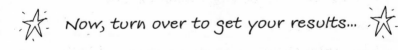 Now, turn over to get your results...

Mostly As: You'd make a great *stylist*! With your finger on the fashion pulse and eye for originality, you can create fab photo-shoot themes and looks. Just go easy on those less style-conscious than you!

Mostly Bs: You'd make a brill *writer*! Sometimes you seem to be hiding in the background but really you're looking and listening, taking everything in. Then you're ready to write it all down and wow your readers!

Mostly Cs: You'd make a fab *photographer*! You have an eye for a picture-perfect shot and a talent for making people feel at ease — so grab your camera now and start snapping!

Totally Secret Info about Kelly McKain

Lives: In a small flat in Chiswick, West London, with a fridge full of chocolate.

Life's ambition: To be a showgirl in Paris 100 years ago. *(Erm, not really possible that one! – Ed.)* Okay, then, to be a writer – so I am actually doing it – yay! And also, to go on a flying trapeze.

Star sign: Capricorn (we're meant to be practical).

Fave colour: Purple.

Fave animal: Monkey.

Ideal pet: A purple monkey.

Fashion shoot fiasco: Leaving my photo-shoot make-up on for a date straight afterwards – and not realizing that in daylight it made me look like a scary clown! Yikes!

Fave hobbies: Hanging out with my BFF and gorge boyf, watching *Friends*, going to yoga and dance classes, and playing my guitar as badly as Lucy's dad!

 Find out more about Kelly at www.kellymckain.co.uk

Have you read all of Lucy's hilarious journals?

Makeover Magic

When a geeky new girl starts at school, style queen Lucy comes up with a fab Makeover Plan to help her fit in.

9780746066898

Fantasy Fashion

Lucy's fave mag is running a comp to design a fantasy fashion outfit and Lucy is determined to win first prize!

9780746066904

Boy Band Blues

Lucy is mega-excited to be styling a boy band for a Battle of the Bands competition – it's just a shame lead singer Wayne is such a big-head!

9780746066911

Star Struck

Lucy's won a part as a film extra and decides she must get her fab design skills noticed on screen – but will the director appreciate her original efforts?

9780746070611

Picture Perfect

Lucy decides to throw a surprise party for Tilda's birthday – but will crossed wires wreck their friendship?

9780746070628

Style School

Lucy sets up a Style School in the loos, but what will happen when the School Uniform Police finds out?

9780746070635

Summer Stars

The girls are thrilled to be going on holiday together, especially as their fave mag is holding a dance competition in the same town!

9780746080177

catwalk crazy

Lucy is putting on a charity show but someone is sabotaging her efforts. Can she track down the culprit and win back her audience before it's too late?

9780746080184

coming soon

Planet Fashion

Tilda's bedroom is a design disaster, until Lucy and Jules give it an eco-friendly makeover. Will their project win them a feature on Tilda's fave TV show, Go Green?

9780746080191

Best Friends Forever

Lucy transforms the boring school disco into a super-stylish High School Prom. But will she find the right boy to make her big red-carpet entrance with?

9780746080207

All priced at £4.99

To Jill and Mike, with thanks for all
your support and enthusiasm
(and the excellent dinners!)

First published in the UK in 2006 by Usborne Publishing Ltd., Usborne
House, 83-85 Saffron Hill, London EC1N 8RT, England. www.usborne.com

Text copyright © Kelly McKain, 2006.
Illustration copyright © Usborne Publishing Ltd., 2006

Illustrations by Vici Leyhane.
Photography: Girl running on beach, page 38: © Ole Graf/zefa/CORBIS.
Girl in sunglasses, page 39 © Emma Rian/zefa/CORBIS.

The name Usborne and the devices ♀ ⊕ are Trade Marks of Usborne
Publishing Ltd.

A CIP catalogue record for this book is available from the British Library.

JFMAM JASOND/08   ISBN 9780746070628   Printed in Great Britain.